Acknowledgments

Before you jump into Maggie's boots and slip into her adventures, there are several people I would like to thank for their help. I am grateful for Muriel Morley's gracious willingness to give me feedback on my manuscript. Muriel's love of writing and her gift for teaching contributed to the quality of this book. Many thanks to my publisher, P. David Smith, who encouraged me to rewrite my manuscript. His own books have helped preserve the history of the San Juan area — helping the tale of this novel to spring up from factual places and events of the time period. Bonnie Beach's professional editing suggestions gave true polish to the final version. Debbie Brockett showed me how to write immediate scenes and, indirectly through her kindness, that an author has an obligation to share her knowledge. Thanks to everyone at Western Reflections whose input played a part in the final draft. Thanks to the following people, who took time to read drafts of the manuscript: Justine Fritzel, Linda Ragel, Rick Ragel, Hazel Stein, Annie Olson, and Kathy Jensen.

Finally, with a thankful heart, I acknowledge the One who renews my strength, allowing me to "soar on wings like eagles."

14.95

MAGGIE'S WAY

The Story of a Defiant Pioneer Woman

By Lucinda Stein

WESTERN REFLECTIONS PUBLISHING COMPANY®

Lake City, CO

ISBN 978-1-932738-21-6

Library of Congress Control Number: 2005921300

Cover and text design: Laurie Goralka Design
Cover illustration by Frederic Remington, *Harpers Weekly*, 1901

Second Edition
Printed in the United States of America

Western Reflections Publishing Company®
P. O. Box 1149
951 N. Highway 149
Lake City, CO 81235
www.westernreflectionspub.com

Author's Note

Women prospectors, miners, and mule skinners were rare in proportion to the male population of the early West, but they did exist. Only a few women moved beyond the traditional domestic role to pursuits of prospecting, packing, or blacksmithing. Early mining towns with unsettled societies allowed more freedom to a woman of this era, if only she had the disposition and yearning for it.

If you dig deep enough into historical accounts, you discover those women who found far different lives for themselves. In Colorado alone, several women appear in the journals of history. Mountain Charley roamed the early mining towns dressed in male attire. Olga Schaaf Little, a German immigrant, packed burros to mines in the La Plata Mountains of southwestern Colorado. Anna Mau prospected in Breckenridge, Colorado. Mrs. Morehouse Mallen, at the age of fifty-eight, left children and grandchildren to prospect in Colorado's Twin Lakes area for twenty-two years.

I have taken the liberty of creating personalities and situations for two real historical people of this time period: Clara Brown and Amos Randall. Otto Mears, Chief Ouray, George Porter, William Freeland, and Thomas Walsh are briefly mentioned in the story and were noted personalities of this time. All the mines mentioned were actual worked mines of this period.

In this era with its rigid cultural expectations, women who pursued unusual occupations were, by far, greater mavericks and freer spirits than any cowboy riding off into the sunset of an old Western movie. To these real women of history, I dedicate this story.

1876-COLORADO TERRITORY

I dragged my eyes from the mud-encrusted toes of the man's boots, past the sinister eyes of the Remington's double barrels aimed at me, to the evil sneer shifting across the man's face. It was the foreman of the mine that I had delivered supplies to earlier. A big, mangy dog growled at his side, its wiry hair matted with mud. As I looked around for a way of escape, I could hear my mother saying, "Maggie O'Malley, what have you gotten yourself into this time?"

"Git down," he bellowed. He thrust the barrels over to my face.

I dismounted and faced the brute. I recalled the man staring at me back at the mine, his dark eyes snaking over my body the entire time. A hawk screamed overhead. My legs grew weak. The blood pounded at my temples. Just then, his ill-behaved mutt of a dog jumped up on him and licked his face. As the man cursed the dog and flailed his arms at the animal, I drew the Colt .44 from beneath my unbuttoned oilskin coat and cocked the revolver. His eyes widened, then locked onto my gun aimed straight at his heart.

"Now, mister," I said. "You might kill me, but you're going down, too. So, I'd back away and let me by."

For a moment he glared at me, as if calculating his odds. At last, he slowly lowered his gun and held up one hand. "Okay, miss. I guess ya're just stubborn enough ta die. Don't do nothin' rash, now . . . I'm leavin'. "

Never taking my eyes off him for an instant, I grasped behind me for the reins of my horse. Leading the mules down the trail, I didn't turn my back on the man until he was out of sight. Then I remounted. My heart raced as I rode back with my gun outstretched in my shaking hand. This was my first brush with danger as a wet-behind-the-ears mule skinner. Only seventeen, I had been warned of the perils of the job by my boss and cajoled by my mother to find a less hazardous job. Unfortunately, it wouldn't be the last time I ran head-on into danger.

Half an hour down the trail, my breathing slowed and I returned my revolver to the stiff, leather holster. Forcing myself to relax, I took in the scenery. The pines jutted up, standing like sentinels on the Rocky Mountain slopes. The aroma of piney sap drifted on the air, filling my nostrils. I had heard of Indians using the sticky pitch of the blue spruce as a poultice for sores. Fat furry marmots or, as some called them, woodchucks scurried above on the rocky outcrops. Frequently, I spotted the signs of mining excavations: mounds of dirt formed below dark, gaping mouths in the earth. These were common monuments to shattered dreams and hopes, but occasionally a fortune was made in developed mines.

Feeling better, I decided not to jeopardize my position as mule skinner by complaining about what had happened. Setting my jaw, I headed the mules back to Dunnick's Freighting at the end of the day. At last, I reached my destination in Ouray, pulling the mule train up to the large sliding double doors.

My boss sauntered up to me. "Everythin' go okay, Maggie?" Jonus asked. The large, black man leaned on the wooden-handled shovel he carried.

"Fine, but dead tired — need a good night's rest." I left, wanting nothing more than to sink into my feather mattress and sleep until dawn.

A few days later Jonas caught me in the middle of mucking out the stables. "Milton Cline came in for a horse yesterday," he said.

My stomach lurched. Cline was the owner of the Micky Breene Mine, the scene of my regrettable encounter. A shiver crawled down my back as the foreman's face appeared in my mind.

"Seems the foreman 'ad problems with too much juice. Cline fired 'im. Said he'd never quite trusted the man."

"I knew there was something about him I didn't like." I hoped Jonas didn't detect the slight waver in my voice. Wouldn't give anyone room to think I couldn't handle myself.

After a few mule trains up the mountains, Dunnick held some confidence in my packing. I no longer worried whether I would be allowed to be a mule skinner. However, a faint flutter in the back of my mind hovered like a bad dream I couldn't shake. Would there be more menacing characters like the foreman? My luck had held out that time, but would it again?

A LONG WAY FROM IRELAND

A pair of rough hands clenched my neck as I slept. My eyes opened in the dim light to find the foreman's cursed face leering down at me. I struggled to breathe. My knee found his groin in one great kick. The pulsing pressure at my neck released. I was halfway to my feet when he grabbed my left leg, and the scuffle continued as we rolled on the ground.

"My word, Maggie, girl," Ma cried, looking down at me.

There I was on the hard wooden floor where I had fallen from my bed. My heart thumped against my chest, and it took a moment to get my bearings. "I'm fine, Ma." I sucked in a deep breath and rubbed my eyes.

"You may have to give up that bowl of chili before bed." Ma shook her head as she descended the creaking stairs to the kitchen.

Another nightmare. The occurrence at the Micky Breene Mine had rattled my resolve to be a mule skinner, but the alternative — the prospect of spending my days cooking, cleaning, and sewing — was nearly as disturbing.

Only a year before when I was seventeen, I had decided to head out across the Colorado Territory. I was already taller than Ma, no doubt due to her good cooking. I kept my thick, dark auburn hair in a braid tucked under a wide-brimmed hat. Ma teased me that I was trying to keep the boys away, because if they ever caught a glimpse of my beautiful hair they would all be after me. I had better things to do than fuss with my hair; if I had any free time, I could be found outdoors riding. Besides, a boy's interest could lead to marriage and that was the last thing on my mind. My face smeared with dirt and my fingernails embedded with red soil, I could often be found working with the horses. The Jacobson's oldest son, Richard, once said, "Maggie O'Malley, you might even be pretty if you would take care with your appearance and weren't so darn independent." Of course, Ma insisted I wash up before every meal, but my looks were the least of my concerns.

Anyway, heading out was an idea quite wedged in my hard head. To tell the truth, if Ma had not agreed, I'm not sure I would have gone. I suppose I will never know because, due to my good luck, Ma accompanied me. To this day, I still don't know why she agreed to such a risky idea coming from one still wet behind the ears.

The tale of how I came to be in this crude mining town, deep in the wildest terrain in all the Rocky Mountains, hinged on decisions my mother made before I was born. Sometimes we forget how our lives build on events that occurred decades before our lifetime. My mother, like countless others from that time, came through many trying experiences. I honestly came by the grit and mettle that have served me so well. My mother's own incredible journey testified to my earliest adventures in life.

My roots stem directly from Ireland, the Emerald Isle, where both my parents were born. However, they met much later on another continent — in a place called the "land of opportunity," America. My mother, Margaret O'Flanagan, grew up in a family of farmers, a people accustomed to working hard for their livelihood. She had often said that the green fields of Ireland were an amazing color, one she had not found in this country in all of her travels. Their home had been a thatched cottage, its walls formed of gathered stone. It had always stayed with me, that strange way they had of heating and cooking. I have spent years cutting and burning wood in the Rockies, so it is a wonder to think a person would dig for their fuel. Using a tool called a slane, she told how they would dig out blocks of peat, laying the sods out to dry in the hot sun.

When my mother was young, the land was owned by British aristocracy, of whom many did not even live in Ireland. The O'Flanagan's farm was no exception. Like all Irish tenants, they detested the landlords who would raise the rent at will, ironically often in proportion to any improvements made by the hardworking people. Times became difficult for the Irish, who could barely feed themselves.

Potatoes, which grew easily even in poor soil, were a staple to the Irish, as bread was to Americans. The Great Famine, which my mother called the "potato famine," began in the year 1845 and lasted for five years. The farmers expected a large harvest that year, making it one of the great ironies of the situation. The abundant crop did indeed materialize but lay rotting in the ground later that summer due to a destructive blight. This blight proved fatal for the following year's crop, and a spore-spreading fungus was diagnosed decades later as the cause of the devastation. In the years that followed, thousands died from starvation and disease. My mother recalled that the famine was not selective in its victims: it felled young men in the prime of life, groped for young mothers needed by their little children, and shook babes straight to the grave.

A peasant who, in desperation, accepted public relief, by law forfeited his holding to his land and thus met with ejection. Landowners enforced country rents on land in January, an unproductive time in the year for the farmer's crops and animals. My mother's parents watched as peasants struggled to keep their harvest of crops or cattle instead of paying rent. Those who retaliated for the injustices were soon sentenced to the silence of the gallows. At the same time, the bustling, noisy seaports filled to the brim with vessels loaded with corn and cattle due for England.

Ma was an easygoing child, eager to please her parents and avert any additional grief to her struggling family, but when she crawled into bed at night, her stomach still growling from the meager proportions of food, she often fell asleep with sour, frustrated tears upon her pillow.

Thus, I learned as a young child the source of Irish enmity against the British people. After the great fire of London, the Irish sent twenty thousand fat cattle for relief; a sum far less came from England and Europe for aid to the suffering Irishmen in 1846. The majority of the gentry went on with the business of shipping harvests to England as if the current suffering and misery were simply not their concern.

Meanwhile, thousands of British soldiers clad in blood-red jackets stood ready to maintain law and order. Men were convicted of killing horses, the crime having been committed to keep from starving, and stealing food became an offense that condemned even the children. The government spent more to issue the official cause of death than to preserve a person's life. The only things overflowing besides the English-bound ships full of food were the decrepit jails and poorhouses.

It was out of the midst of this travail that my mother's young life was spun. Disease, death, and heartache were close kin to the misery of famine. Ma's father had already died of typhus. Jonathan, a young brother half crazed with grief and fear, fled to England by hiding on board a ship after the death of his father. They had had no word from him.

❧ 3 ❧

THE GREAT VOYAGE

1846-47: Margaret's Story

Margaret clung to her sixteen-year-old brother, Patrick, after the death of her father. The strapping young lad was dark haired, striking, and full of youthful confidence. Patrick took on the role of the household without hesitation. Yet, even with this heavy responsibility on one so young, he found time for his little sister.

He called out one day, in a no-nonsense tone of voice. "Little Margaret, come out and do your chores."

Nine-year-old Margaret skipped out the door of the cottage to encounter showers of freshly picked flower petals raining over her head. The sound of his young sister's squeal of laughter at such moments tickled Patrick.

"Patrick, my devilish, bothersome brother," she cried, as her rosy cheeks formed a great smile.

A few months later, Patrick killed and butchered a British gentry's cow for food for the family. He came up missing shortly afterwards. Margaret never heard from her beloved brother again.

By 1847, landowners found it more economical to send tenants to America than to continue to subsidize the government-required poorhouses. So came the day that poorhouse workers pulled Margaret and her mother out to speak to the priest in charge. He told them the landowner had procured their passage to America. Squinting in the intense sunlight, Margaret felt the pressure of her mother's hand upon her slim shoulder.

"Thank you, Father," Margaret's mother whispered, pulling her shawl snugly against the chill of the morning air. The harshness of forty-seven years of hard living had weathered her appearance not unlike a windswept tree battered beside the sea. Her small-framed body had grown thin and frail. Silver framed her strong cheekbones, the lines in her face records of a lifetime of struggles.

Margaret's mother had been sickly for weeks, so she had the priest make arrangements for Margaret to travel with a neighbor who had also received free passage. She promised to follow shortly when her health improved. Margaret had never traveled alone. She had never been so far as to the village without a brother along. The young girl blinked back the moisture forming in her eyes as she walked slowly back into the building, supporting her mother in her weakened state. The cold-edged wind stole Margaret's hot tears.

She stood on the shore, looking up at the sky. Heavy, gray clouds hung low and ominous over the ship's masts, like an evil omen threatening to stir up high, wild waves in the ocean cauldron. A bone-chilling spray blew across the water, slapping her face and reaching down her thin neck. Margaret drew her wool cloak together, fastening it closed. She pulled the coarse hood of the garment over the damp locks of her dark hair. The storm did not disparage her spirits. There was no looking back now. Her father, rest his soul, would forever lie a true Irishman in the native soil of the country he loved, but the songs she had heard sung in the harbor town in the last few days spoke of promise. "They say there's land and work for all, And the sun shines always there." Surely, though, he would be happy that she and Mother now had hope of a brighter future in America.

A mere ten years old, Margaret clutched the voucher with "Passage to America" printed on it in bold, black letters. Her other small hand held a tight bundle of clothes gathered with a cloth and tied with a thin rope. Some dried beef, tea, and oatcakes wrapped in brown butcher's paper rode in the center of the bundle. Also, tucked inside was an unopened letter from Mother that she had been sworn to open only upon arrival in America. Standing behind the neighbor she accompanied — a woman named Mrs. O'Neil — and Mrs. O'Neil's three children, Margaret waited in line to exchange the voucher for a ticket.

Four hours later, they boarded the tender, which would take them to the steamship *Washington*, moored further out. The small O'Neil boy sat in front of Margaret. Whenever he leaned too far over the side, she grabbed his coat collar. "Settle yourself," she reprimanded.

"Spittle." He poked his small, pink tongue out at her.

Margaret responded as if the act was as inconsequential as a fly buzzing in the distance. She tilted her head against the spray of the seawater while still keeping the boy in sight. Mrs. O'Neil did not seem to be aware of what her children were doing, her eyes staring straight ahead. Halfway to the *Washington*, Margaret braved a look at the ship. Sailors unfurled the sails at each of the three masts. The great side wheels rose midway on the side of the vessel.

When they arrived at the ship, they were the last boarded, along with the other steerage passengers. The landowners purchased passage for their tenants with the cheapest rate possible. Unlike their poorer shipmates, first-class passengers were the first boarded and the first to disembark the vessel at the end of the journey. Standing on the deck, Margaret wiped the biting cold moisture from her face with her coat sleeve. She looked back as Ireland vanished in a late spring fog, the apparition constricting her heart with its heavy fist.

Margaret entered the foreboding, dank darkness of the lowest deck of the steamship with trepidation.

"To the back," a scruffy sailor snarled. One eye stared out faded and lifeless below a ragged scar. The other black-umber eye pierced the object of its aim.

Margaret avoided the man's eyes and turned her face aside, trying to elude the sour, musky stench of the sailor.

"Hurry now." He shoved on Margaret's back, causing her to stumble into the O'Neil child walking ahead of her. Little Brian fell and began sobbing. Margaret helped him up and hurried him along.

"Shhh, it's okay, now," she said. Margaret forgot her apprehension and glared at the man, but he was busy herding the other passengers.

When her eyes adjusted to the dimness, she saw row upon row of narrow bunks. They would spend the majority of the voyage within these cramped spaces. Margaret shared her bunk with two of the O'Neil children. The sailors placed the women and children at the back of the ship. Seasickness overcame many of the passengers that first day as the result of the constant motion of the waves breaking against the ship's frame. Margaret was uncertain if she became nauseous due to seasickness or from the sight, sound, and smell of others retching all around her.

On warmer days, the heat combined with the odor of too many human bodies crowded together. The crew forbade washing of bodies, as drinkable water was limited. At night, there was never silence due to the constant sounds of coughing, snoring, tossing, and turning. Margaret felt imprisoned.

She spent much of her time entertaining the three O'Neil children, inventing wild tales of adventure or creating simple games to play. It became trying as she spent countless hours keeping the children occupied in order to prevent squabbles, but it kept her mind from wandering too much. Mrs. O'Neil wasn't the neighbor she remembered back on the farm; she never smiled anymore and became cross with the children.

No more than one meal was served a day, usually a tin mug of thin soup of indeterminable origin, more of a broth, with one piece of hard bread or biscuit. Occasionally it would be varied with a cup of stew flavored by some oddly-textured meat. The steward hurried past each bunk distributing the meager food like a farmer feeding his animals, concerned only that they make it to market. Hundreds of steerage passengers shared seven lavatories, creating waiting lines that lasted for hours. A person could not rely on the natural timing of the body. Often Margaret fell to begging.

"Please, ma'am," she said, "he's too little to hold it much longer." Sometimes a passenger would respond in kindness and allow them to move forward in the line. Other times, it was allowed begrudgingly; once, with a cuff to the head by a bitter-faced crone.

Privacy was not available to the lower-class passengers. Although the women were separated from the male passengers, the crew came and went at odd times, often with no reason to be there, especially in the early morning when women were dressing. It became common for crewmen to grope the young women, but it was dangerous to protest too much before they were safely in America. Some of the men threatened to prevent the women's admission to the new country. Luckily for Margaret, her young body had not yet begun maturing and thus did not draw any such attention.

Although multitudes fled from the ravished Irish countryside, ill fortune continued to plague them. Besides their meager parcels, passengers carried disease, and its morbid companion, death, ever beckoned. Dysentery, typhus, and cholera were common on the voyage. The same basin used for hand washing was also a receptacle for the results of seasickness. Many deaths occurred on board. Bodies were hurled into the sea, preferably at night, to spare the first-class passengers the reality of death that followed the ship like an ever-looming specter. It was no wonder the all-too-knowing Irish gave the name "coffin ships" to the vessels.

Toward the end of the journey, a trunk fell on seven-year-old Ben O'Neil's head during a day of violent waves. After the accident, he became sluggish and his appetite diminished. Mrs. O'Neil focused her attention on him thereafter, ignoring the other children and placing more of the burden on Margaret.

Resigned to the fact that her tears would go unnoticed, Margaret stoically labored through the days, each a repeat of the one before: combing the children's hair, accompanying them to the lavatory, thinking of new games to play, and singing them to sleep at night. As a person lost in the woods, she realized that the lone option was to move on. Late at night, however, in those short moments of fitful sleep, Margaret dreamt of the sweet-grass scent of Mother's skin and implored her to come, to be there for her, holding her once again and singing Irish folk songs to her as she used to do at bedtime. Young Margaret endured sixteen days and nights of this deplorable voyage and arrived at last on the shores of America with her health intact, though weak and tried it was. Never in her life had she waited for anything as much as for her mother to join her in this new world.

4

THE NEW COUNTRY

Margaret's Story

Young Margaret fidgeted, unable to sit still any longer as she waited to bid farewell to the dark, odoriferous confinement of the steerage level. The *Washington* had dropped anchor off the shores of New York hours before, but the anxious passengers had no choice but to wait: first-class passengers were the first to disembark. When at last the steerage passengers were allowed above deck, they were required to go through slow, exhausting lines past American doctors who allowed the reasonably healthy to proceed.

Margaret and the O'Neil family stood on the main deck breathing fresh air for the first time in over two weeks. White clouds floated high in the azure sky. The sun glimmered over the water as if to welcome them from their prison. A myriad of ships of all types and sizes surrounded the *Washington*, some moored, many just entering the crowded harbor. Margaret followed Mrs. O'Neil and the children down the gangplank. Three-year-old Brian clung to her hand now that they had become friends after the long days down in the belly of the ship.

Large warehouses rose from the shore where crates and boxes were stacked. Everywhere the eye could see, men were constantly moving or stacking loads. Now they once again stood and waited, this time for Mr. O'Neil to find them out of this great crowd of disembarking passengers. Some young boys about Margaret's age hurried through the crowds offering their assistance to the new arrivals. What most surprised her was that they spoke with an Irish brogue. When one of the lads stopped and asked Mrs. O'Neil if she needed any directions for accommodations, she rebuffed him.

"Go on with ya now, leave us alone! Get outta here," Mrs. O'Neil barked.

Margaret thought it rude, especially to fellow countrymen who were trying to welcome them to the new country. Later she heard Mrs. O'Neil explain to another woman that her husband had warned her about the "runners" who were hired to direct passengers to overpriced accommodations or transportation.

They sat on their meager bundles of clothing, removing their cloaks in the warm air. The balmy rays of sunshine spread over Margaret's skin like exotic oils. She breathed deeply of the sweet, fresh air. An occasional whiff of pipe tobacco, the familiar aroma of horseflesh from carriages arriving in the distance, and the reek of washed up ocean vegetation mingled in the air. Margaret studied the tall buildings in the distance, as the loud bustle of the nearby streets pervaded the scene.

Forty minutes later, Mr. O'Neil arrived. It was the first genuine smile Margaret had seen on the Mrs.' face since the voyage. The other children waited shyly for their father's attention. Little Brian, the youngest O'Neil, held back when his father's arms reached out to him. Margaret whispered in his ear, "Go ahead. It's okay; it's your Pa." Brian looked over at his smiling mother and ran to his father's arms, the rest laughing at the scene. Margaret held back hot tears. Her own father's arms would never reach for her again. Finally, Mrs. O'Neil introduced Margaret, as her husband did not recognize the growing daughter of his old neighbors. He patted her on the shoulder and thanked her for her help with the children.

She shadowed the small entourage that made up the O'Neil family, afraid to become lost in the noisy crowd. They walked unsteadily, weakened from the inactivity and poor food on the voyage. They passed huge open markets of food and walked down large tree-lined streets. Soon they turned off into a narrow, unkempt lane. Margaret tried to pay attention and not risk falling behind, which was a trial with all the new sights and people that competed for her attention. Outside a three-story brick building, Margaret was left with the children while Mr. and Mrs. O'Neil took Ben inside. Mr. O'Neil had decided Ben needed medical attention. Forty minutes in the hot sun were nothing compared to the dank, suffocating heat of the steerage class of the ship. Along with the wonderful sunshine, there was so much to take in: people of all nationalities speaking different languages while carts, horses, and stray dogs paraded past.

At last, the O'Neils returned without Ben, who remained in the infirmary's care, and the small party continued. Finally, they arrived at the row house that would become Margaret's home for the next two years. The four-story tenement house was indistinguishable from the others except for the sign: 57 Orchard Street. Their three-room apartment was located on the second floor. The contractors created the buildings with the intention of packing in as many immigrants as possible for the maximum rental fees for the owner.

To her surprise, Margaret soon discovered that they would not be living in the three-room accommodations alone. They lived with a young married couple — the Shannons — and their relatives: Mrs. Shannon's female cousin, and Mr. Shannon's sister and brother-in-law. Eleven people lived in the cramped quarters. It was made bearable only by the variety of their job shifts. It turned out the reported "streets paved in gold" would be won only by long hours of sweat and strain. New York was a great city teeming with immigrants from many countries, and it was within the sweating, bustling, trying hopefulness of this generation that young Margaret began her life in America.

The first meal that Mrs. O'Neil prepared in America included oxtail soup, fresh bread, corned beef, potatoes, and carrots. Margaret ate the dinner with relish as if she was one of the richest women in America. After so much meagerness, this made her feel as if she had found the pot of gold. Mr. O'Neil worked down below in the storefront of the building, managing the small dry goods store for the owner of the tenement. For cooking the daily meals, Mrs. O'Neil collected a monthly fee from the others who shared the apartment. The Shannons both worked: he at a warehouse down by the wharves, she as a seamstress at a clothing factory. Mr. Shannon's brother-in-law joined him at the warehouse within a few weeks; his sister waited to get on at the clothing factory. Someone was coming or going at all hours of the day and night. Margaret eventually grew used to the noise and slept through it all. She took care of the children and helped with the food preparation. Her pay was all the food she could eat, along with free room and board.

After two busy days of settling in, the O'Neils paid a visit to the hospital to check on Ben. Two hours later, they returned, their faces ashen and rigid with tension. Mary Shannon darted to Mrs. O'Neil, and Mr. O'Neil escorted them into a nearby bedroom, shutting the door behind them. Margaret tried to distract the children with a game while her mind and ears fixed on the next room. She distinctly heard Mrs. O'Neil say repeatedly, "I know he's not dead. They're lying! I know they are!"

"Shh, the children will hear," Mr. O'Neil admonished her.

After a few minutes, Mr. O'Neil came out of the room. Mr. Shannon took his arm and directed him to the hall. The door slammed behind them. Margaret could not stand the tension and moved nearer to the door. While the children exuberantly played hide and seek around the small flat, Margaret placed an ear up to the door. She could make out a few of the words: "no body . . . claim it was put in a pauper's grave . . . lying, I tell you." In a few minutes, Mr. O'Neil and Mr. Shannon headed

Maggie's Way

down the stairway with firm footsteps. The irreconcilable sounds of children playing remained along with grief-stricken cries escaping from behind the bedroom door.

Crying that she thought would never end.

5

THE MALLOY EMPLOYMENT AGENCY

Margaret's Story

Later that night, Mr. Shannon gathered everyone together, with the obvious exception of Mrs. O'Neil, to break the news of Ben's death. Margaret noticed the looks that passed between Mr. O'Neil and Mr. Shannon when the word "death" was used. The younger children did not display any emotion until they understood death meant never seeing or playing with brother Ben again. Margaret's blood froze in her veins. For years to come, she feared getting seriously ill and never returning from a place that did not give the body back to the family. When she was older, she heard tales of stolen immigrant children used in child labor racketeering. Many took advantage of the immigrants who lacked money, influence, and sometimes even the English language to protect them. In such a large city as New York, tracing such travesties proved impossible.

A week later, Margaret realized she had forgotten her mother's letter, tucked beneath her bedding on the floor. Each evening she had been too weary to read the message. Then, of course, there had been Ben. Mother. . . everything would be better when Mother joined her. Before the children awakened that morning, she tore open the envelope. She devoured the letter.

Dearest Margaret,

By now, you will be standing on America's soil with your future before you. I must confess I never planned on joining you, as I have known for a while that my illness was without cure. I could not risk you refusing to leave out of duty to me. Who knows how long the offer for your passage would have stood, and my days are numbered.

My dear girl, remember your father and I loved you. You have the blood of the O'Flanagans running through your veins, thus you have more than enough strength and courage to carry you through life. Seek what you desire in your new land of opportunity and be happy in all circumstances.

Go with God,
Mother

In Margaret's short life, she had seen enough of tragedy to accept it as common as the dawn appearing every morning. Accepting the harshness of life, however, did not prevent horrible emptiness, pain, and despair. For the next year, Margaret staggered through life numb to emotion, the deep human instinct for survival prodding her to carry on. Perhaps as bad as the loss was the isolation she felt, for although the O'Neils did not treat her badly, she was not part of their family. Life was too hard for them to take time to embrace another child, especially when they were dealing with the loss of their own.

Two years later, Margaret became a "Bridgette," what women in domestic service were commonly called because the job became so identified with Irish women. Even if the girl was not Irish, the name stuck. Margaret made friends with another young Irish girl named Mary in her tenement building. The two decided to attend the Molloy Employment Agency of Young Ladies. Here, they received instruction for five months, learning the proper behavior, expectations, and job requirements to be domestic help in New York.

The owner of the agency, Mrs. Malloy, was an older woman with years of experience in domestic help: downstairs, upstairs, kitchens, and sculleries. She now made a comfortable living training these new immigrants and garnishing their wages for up to a year. In addition, every evening Mrs. Malloy taught the girls rudimentary skills in reading and writing.

Margaret was eventually placed in an upper-class home. That first day driving up in the carriage sent for her, she was amazed at the huge house with its groomed lawn. She would never see the entire expanse of the building, since she was but a kitchen servant. What she could glimpse through the large doors of the dining room would be all she would ever observe. The position included room and board. She shared a small room just off the kitchen with Martha, the stout spinster cook. The work was demanding and inexhaustible.

Every two weeks she enjoyed a day off. She would catch a ride into the business district with the house's coachman as he left to run errands. She often met Mary when their days off corresponded. Her wages were six dollars a month, but, due to the agency's fees, she would see just three dollars per month for a year, most of which she saved. One of the first things Margaret bought for herself was a hat. In Ireland, only women of high social status wore hats, usually the English landowners' wives, but in America a shawl draped over one's head clearly identified the immigrant. To wear a hat was to step out of the ranks of peasant, even if for a brief time on one's day off.

"Ain't you the smart one," Mary said, as she caught sight of her friend.

The two young women stood in front of a mirror in the women's apparel section of the large store. They tried on hat after hat, searching for just the right one. Margaret had donned a soft blue hat. Mary was right — the color drew her blue eyes into focus and the angle of the brim pronounced her high cheekbones. Her fine-textured skin blushed with the giddiness of their carefree shopping trip.

"I am, at that, my dear." Margaret's eyebrows lifted in a theatrical expression. It was for these trips on her day off that Margaret lived. She never tired of seeing all the wondrous things that this new country had to offer: open-air markets overflowing with novel varieties of fruits and vegetables; store windows displaying the latest fashionable bonnets, muffs, and velvet dresses; and exquisite windows revealing everything from delicate knickknacks to stained-glass lamps. It was indeed a wonderful city.

However, Margaret also saw signs reading "No Irish Need Apply" frequently displayed on doors and windows. America, it appeared, was distrustful of her nationality. The Irish usually took the poorest jobs and Americans resented them. Many viewed Irish poverty as part of the Irish character rather than as a result of circumstances. They held the Irish reputation for drink against them (as if they were the only nationality to partake) while the Protestant majority of the country felt threatened by their beliefs and way of life. Though the ability of the Irish to organize themselves in religion and labor was merely to improve their lot in life, many saw this as a conspiratorial act against the rest of the country. Margaret's prospects in the "land of opportunity" had its limits.

6

FIRE IN MY HEAD

Ma said it was due to my good-natured, obedient manner even as a young child that enabled her to work as a live-in servant. She could always find something simple for me to play with and I would keep myself occupied for hours, leaving Ma free to complete her work. Of course, I was always within view of her watchful eyes. In the evenings, she took time to read to me, or we would stroll down the dirt road, an occasional bird song breaking out of the evening's hush. I remembered watching colors building into a sunset.

"Maggie, watch closely as the Lord paints the sky," she whispered. She wrapped her arms around my shoulders, as the colors of the sky reflected in her eyes. My young mind filled with wonder at the unfolding show.

Ma's days started before dawn and stretched into the evening. Looking back, I realize she must have been exhausted.

By the age of five, I helped in the kitchen in small ways. While I buttered the bread or stirred the batter with the big wooden spoon, I felt important as I helped my mother. By the time I was ten, I knew how to cook a simple meal. I'm grateful that I learned how to cook, since good food is one thing we never stop appreciating, but every chance I had I would hightail it for outside. The family Ma worked for, the Jacobsons, acquired land outside Denver. As Mr. Jacobson's banking assets increased, an impressive second home was built on the acreage. We spent many weekends and summers there, and I grew to love the outdoors with all its smells, sounds, and creatures. Ma said I was a true Irishman in the way I loved the country.

Mrs. Jacobson was a horsewoman and raised Tennessee Walkers. My love of animals revealed itself at age nine when I begged to help care for the horses. Mrs. Jacobson allowed me to brush down the horses after her rides. I loved the soft brush of their velvet mouth over my palm as I gave them oats. By ten years, I rode the horses that needed exercising, tracing the wide circle of the corral. Everyone said I was a natural, but I give credit to Henry Randall, the stable hand, who taught me most of what I learned about horses. He showed me how to gain a horse's trust. I moved about in the corral at first, avoiding directly walking up to the horse or even making eye contact. I spoke softly and calmly as I strolled around. When I rode, Henry taught me to use my body to "talk" to the animal and communicate naturally using slight pressure at the right place at the right time. Only then was I ready for the final requirement, according to Henry: earning the right to be in charge by gaining the horse's respect. Nothing he taught me has ever been proven wrong.

Turning seventeen brought grand thoughts into my head. I got the idea to travel out West, inadvertently, through Henry, or more accurately, his brother, Amos. For a month, I had taken over Henry's duties while he recovered from the mumps. I would have done it for nothing since I liked Henry, but, at his insistence, I finally agreed to take half of his wages (I knew he needed the rest for doctoring). I delighted at getting away from dreary housework. This was the beginning of knowing I did not want to spend my life as a domestic. Amos Randall came visiting from Denver on and off over the next few weeks to see his ailing brother. He was a small man in stature; gray hair feathered through his sideburns, and his strong angled face had a no-nonsense quality that fit his wiry body. That is when I began to see a world bigger than what my seventeen years had shown me. Amos was an old bachelor with a general store in the city. With no family to tie him down, he planned to follow the prospectors to the western part of the Colorado Territory.

"New settlements need supplies," he said, as his faded blue-gray eyes lit up. "With people strikin' it rich, I'd charge higher prices in that far-flung area. In my spare time, I'd try a little prospectin', too."

Amos had heard the rumors of new mineral sightings far to the west. The rumbling excitement of the news had its effect. Amos was in the process of selling his place of business and supplying a small wagon train of goods, which he would use in his new store.

Ma revealed to me then that she knew more about the world than I had figured. She told me that when my father and she were on their way to Denver City, then part of the Kansas Territory, a flood of prospectors had already streamed to the Front Range. The rich minerals on the eastern slope of the Rocky Mountains were soon limited in proportion to the tens of thousands of prospectors and their numerous filed claims. By 1861, this part of the country was reorganized into the Colorado Territory, and I discovered that the tide of prospectors had been moving further west into this land ever since.

That was when a fire was lit in my head. People always needed horses to get around (this was where I hoped to come in), and new towns with hardworking, hungry miners always needed feeding (where Ma would come in). Although the area was newly discovered, eventually it would be opened up to homesteading. Maybe Ma and I could homestead.

I approached Amos with the idea of accompanying him.

"I could help with your animals on the way, and my ma is a great cook," I said.

He laughed as if I was saying silly, childish things. Then his face turned solemn.

"This ain't no trip for the fainthearted," Amos quipped. "I don't need no women slowin' me down and bein' a hindrance."

I stood up and straightened my shoulders back. My chin jutted up. "I do not come from fainthearted stock," I retorted. "My family came out here in a wagon from back East and knew more than their share of tough times. Moreover, I'm not afraid of hard work or getting my hands dirty." My hands on my hips, I glared at the man.

The old fool stopped and took a good look at me. Then he roared with laughter.

"Ask Henry how I work with animals," I continued, as I stood my ground.

Henry backed me up with a smile. "It's true, Amos. Maggie's a hard worker. A real natural with animals. I couldn't 'ave done a better job myself this last month. Moreover, that piece of pie you just 'et was the work of her mother, Margaret. But then again, I'd sure hate to lose those good vittles. Maybe it'd be best if you'd go alone, Amos."

It was Ma's cooking that persuaded old Amos to take two women on his journey after all. Ma was my good fortune.

7

NEW PROSPECTS

Margaret's Story

Margaret toiled for nine long years as a domestic. She was a hardworking girl who grew into a capable young woman. After five years in the same household, she worked her way up to cook. She was offered the position when the overweight cook died of a long-persisting heart problem. She felt Providence finally shining down on her life. She was able to save an extra three dollars every month with the increased wages.

Margaret and best friend Mary were not in any hurry to marry. They had seen the fate of married women at the tenement who, out of necessity, could not work but had to remain home to care for the many children the marriage bed produced. Frequently the husband drank away much of the needed money for the family, never improving their lot.

However, in 1857 on the eve of the New Year, Margaret did succumb to matrimony at the age of twenty-two. Irish blood flowed through the veins of Thomas O'Malley who, like herself, had come over the Atlantic in answer to the beckoning new life. He had the bright red hair that people associate with the Irish, but Margaret often boasted that she had the dark hair of the real Irish. It was a common joke between them: Who was more Irish. Margaret claimed red hair came from the Danes who invaded Ireland centuries before and intermarried with the Irish.

Thomas had been the groundskeeper for several years, arriving a year before Margaret. He was three years older. They did not come to speaking terms until Margaret became head of the kitchen, and thus became the woman to woo for an extra slice of fresh pie or other delight. The fact that both were striving for a better life and both were Irish helped bring them together. Their friendship grew slowly, and Margaret observed how, like herself, Thomas labored and saved for the future. This, along with his good-natured ways and friendly smile, captured her heart.

"That Thomas O'Malley is easy on the eyes," Margaret said. She spoke out loud to herself, with a twinkle in her eyes. Then, her cheeks became pink as wild roses. She spun around to the stove and stirred the soup with needless vigor.

After their marriage, Margaret moved into the groundskeeper's cottage in the back. Though it was small on space, it was a luxury to have the privacy of a separate building.

Margaret was an excellent cook, and one of her specialties was her bread. By July of that year, she was rising plump and soft like her famous bread dough. In that day, proper women recorded the birth of their children as if they miraculously appeared out of thin air, but those who lived closer to nature and were accustomed to seeing animals give birth were not embarrassed with their pregnancies as other women might be.

Within these months of anticipating the beginning of their own family, Thomas's thoughts began to swell like his wife's womb. On trips into the city, he heard the glorious promises of "twice the money to be made" and "acres of land to be claimed beyond what the eye could see." He was full of dreams. It was not difficult to persuade Margaret, who dreamed of ground she could call her own without any landowners to answer to. It was easy at this time in Margaret's life to dream of infinite possibilities.

In the quiet hours of the morning, a baby was born late November of 1858 in the groundskeeper's cottage. Thomas insisted that the babe be given his wife's name, Margaret. However, he soon nicknamed the infant Maggie. He was fond of calling her "Wee little Maggie Margaret."

In March 1859, the O'Malleys set out on their quest for a new life. The first part of the journey was grand, Margaret later reported, as they boarded a train which would take them all the way to St. Joseph, Missouri. The railroad had recently finished the rails to that point. On Washington's birthday the previous month, an engineer had emptied a jug of water from the Mississippi River into the chocolate-colored Missouri in commemoration of the feat. The papers had read: "Two major rivers now linked by rail!" At three-and-a-half months of age, infant Maggie accompanied them on the expedition westward.

During the next few weeks, they spent much of their hard-earned savings. The first thing purchased was a canvas-covered wagon in which they packed all their supplies for the journey. It was built of seasoned hardwood to withstand the tests of temperature and moisture. Doubly thick canvas made of oiled cloth provided a roof over this contraption, which would serve both as sleeping quarters and supply wagon.

Thomas and Margaret packed pound upon pound of flour, bacon and other salted meat, coffee, sugar, salt, beans, rice, dried fruits and vegetables, tallow, and pickles, along with bedding, warm clothing, rifles, shot, and powder. The Missouri River marked the edge of civilization and the people packed accordingly.

St. Joseph was one of the towns referred to as "jumping-off" places along the Missouri River. Hundreds of other emigrants were also preparing their wagons, waiting for early April snows to melt enough to begin their journey. The couple met many people there and joined a large group of families with similar goals of homesteading out West.

On April 5, the wagons pulled out. Tar buckets hung on their sides, and ropes secured spare parts such as wagon tongues, spokes, axles, and wheels. Items were packed under the wagon wherever space would allow. Four oxen pulled the O'Malley's wagon, but up to six oxen were used by families whose loads included treasured furniture.

On the first day of travel, Margaret knew she must put the ease and comfort of travel on the luxurious train behind her. The rhythm of the oxen hooves beat relentlessly into Margaret's head as the animals continuously provoked clouds of dust. The eternal swatting of flies had already become tiresome, and they had only begun their journey. Sweat began to form above her brow; it soon rolled down and stained the dusty film veiling her face. Mrs. Molloy would be appalled, she who so impressed upon them the need to maintain a spotless purity in personal appearance and clothing. There was a certain satisfaction, however, in knowing she was no longer anyone's servant.

Several days passed with the cyclic creaking of the wooden wheels ever turning. "Prairie Schooner" is what the travelers often called the covered wagon. Schooners . . . like the sailing vessel on Margaret's voyage to America. The two modes of travel had a lot in common, she

thought absently . . . hot and dirty . . . and, like the wave-tossed ship, the rough, jarring wagons brought nausea to anyone with a predisposition to motion sickness. Depending on the terrain, weather, amount of sickness, and availability of water, the wagons traveled twelve to twenty-four miles a day. The vast expanse of the land worked greatly on Margaret's mind; the barrenness of the land brought doubts. Would their destination prove better than this? Had she let the emotions of love boggle her mind? How well, after all, did she know this head-in-the-sky Irishman? Moreover, she was encumbered with an infant who demanded continual care! Had she lost all common sense and wisdom?

With a great sigh, Margaret wondered how had she allowed herself to get in this position.

Maggie's Way

8

WESTWARD VENTURE OR FOLLY?

Margaret's Story

Margaret kept her thoughts to herself and reasoned it was too late to turn back now, folly that it might be. She tried to cheer herself with the fact that they were making progress, no matter the scenery remained the same as yesterday. Many had already preceded them on this pathway called the Overland Trail. Each day brought them a little further west. They spent their nights sleeping on the floor of the wagon on a hair mattress topped with a feather-filled ticking. In the evening, sleep overpowered the exhausted travelers while the men took turns standing guard.

Women bonded on the trail out of sheer necessity. Out on the open prairie with no trees for privacy for basic bodily functions, the women's long, full skirts served as curtains for each other. Many women on the journey were pregnant at the start of the trip and relied on the other women when their time came. While the men were brimming with the excitement of their grand adventure, it was a most inopportune time in the lives of their wives: childcare, pregnancy, and childbirth in the middle of nowhere for six to eight months of exhausting travel and hardships. Thomas O'Malley was a good and decent man. He never considered starting the trip before the baby was born proper. It was common for many men to give no thought to what their pregnant wives would have to endure on such a grueling trip.

Cooking was a challenge for Margaret, despite her experience as a domestic. She now battled wind, rain, and smoke-filled eyes while preparing meals. When camped by creeks, the women scoured the banks for branches and trees that had not been stripped by previous wagon trains. Often, though, trees and bushes were not in sight, so the women and children collected large quantities of weeds or dry buffalo chips to maintain a fire for cooking. They had to squat or stoop over the fire to cook, and water had to be hauled over long distances. Women's work began before dawn in order to ensure the wagon train an early start for the day.

The wagon train crossed many rivers throughout the journey. Trappers or, at times, Indians ran the ferries at the crossings for five dollars a wagon and fifty cents for each head of oxen. These were the first

Indians they had ever seen, and they were grateful that a previous encounter with a trapper had enlightened them about their culture. It was an ancient Indian custom to exchange gifts in greeting, though many emigrants mistook it for begging. Margaret tried to be prepared with a kerchief, piece of cloth, or item of food for these moments. She, who had experienced the disdain often shown to new immigrants in New York, saw past the dark skin and unusual clothing. She had compassion for a people who watched strangers week by week conquer their land. The Indians they met as they traveled were friendly, but, in a few years, violence would become commonplace. By that time, the native's patience and tolerance had been exploited too often.

At crossings without ferries, everything in the wagons had to be unloaded and placed on rafts and reloaded on the other side. The men used the tar from the buckets hung on the wagon sides for caulking the slats of the wagon. They heard of many men who had drowned at a swollen stream in full view of friends and family.

Windstorms, lightening, hail, rain, and mud were other natural elements to battle. Dead cattle, horses, and overworked oxen often lay rotting, the stench rising in the heat of the day. Margaret solemnly observed graves along the trail, seen far too frequently. If not dug deep enough, wolves would dig into the mounds. Dysentery, often called the bloody flux, was common among the travelers since the quality and quantity of water varied throughout the trip. Deadly typhoid, measles, and smallpox also brought their toll on the emigrants. Cholera, which many of the homesteaders thought they were fleeing, was actually carried by the multitudes across the continent. Beds and clothing discarded or burning along the trail indicated death from these diseases.

Although the women submitted to these hardships with courage in their hearts, many determined the westward venture of their husbands was exacting too supreme an expense in human life. Margaret watched the suffering of fellow travelers on the overland journey, wishing she could erase the sight of it all. How many women wished they had never come?

Along with the other men, Thomas caught news of the "Pike's Peak Diggings." They began to fancy finding gold alongside their original objective of homesteading. A third of the families in their train broke off from the Overland Trail in the Nebraska Territory in mid-August. Margaret was beginning to agree with the women that there was something to this Gold Fever. It seemed to addle the men's brains with its lure of quick riches, but if Thomas kept to their original plan of homesteading and ranching, she would keep quiet.

Maggie's Way

Their eventual destination would be Denver City. There they would find supplies, make needed repairs to the wagons, investigate areas for homesteading, and hear fresh news about the most recent bonanzas. They followed the South Platte River south to land that was then still part of the Kansas Territory.

Soon after turning off the Overland Trail, Thomas was troubled with a slight fever. Margaret, in optimism, thought it was just the effects of the blasted dysentery that had plagued them both on and off during the trip. The fever grew worse until she at last was driving the oxen by herself.

Cholera took Thomas O'Malley's life two days before reaching their destination. The sideboards of the wagon served as the makings for a makeshift coffin for his body. In September of 1859, Margaret arrived in Denver City a widow with a young infant. Like the dried up creek beds seen along her journey, all hopes and dreams had evaporated.

Traveling by covered wagon to the West.
Drawn by Frenzeny and Tavenier.
Harper's Weekly, April 4, 1874.

Maggie's Way

9

DENVER CITY

Margaret's Story

The irony of Margaret's dreams of a new life stared her in the face, but she carried with her, from the years of being a new immigrant, the fatalism of "what would be, would be." Although the marriage was brief, no one ever matched up to Thomas O'Malley. She always counted herself extremely fortunate to have found a man of such character.

The men in the wagon train helped Margaret sell the wagon and oxen. Since they had not transported furniture, she was left with clothing, bedding, and a few pots and pans. She refused one family's offer to stay with them until she was settled. She was not about to be a burden to anyone, and the sooner she got on with her life, whatever that might entail, the better for everyone. Pride can be a sign of strong character, but sometimes it turns out to be just plain poor judgment.

Armed with two satchels of what belongings she had left in the world on one arm, and a baby growing ever heavier in her other arm, Margaret slumped on the rough wooden bench outside a general store. She considered her options, something she should have sorted out by now, but Thomas's sudden death was numbing. She considered returning to the position of a domestic servant.

Maggie's cry of hunger brought her back to the present moment. She had not yet figured out where she would stay tonight, but at this moment she needed to nurse her child. Struggling with the two heavy satchels and the crying child, she walked around the corner of the building looking for a private spot. A small creek flowed in the near distance, lined with a high bank of trees and willows. There she found a convenient place out of sight from the buildings on the hill above. She opened the bodice of her dress just enough to let the child suckle.

She forced herself back to deciding her life's course — their lives depended on it. House servant or cook? She would have to find the area of town where the wealthy resided: the businessmen, bankers, and lawyers, those who could afford the luxury of servants. Then her thoughts went back to Maggie. Soon she would be walking, getting into everything. Who would hire her with a tot whining and tugging at her skirts?

This should not be happening; she was a married woman . . . even yet, she had trouble accepting Thomas's death as a fact. She expected him to come around the corner at any moment, to tell her everything would be all right.

Tears, which up until this time had been held back, now poured forth. The sound was barely audible, but the scene had not gone undetected. High above on the hill, a dark face saw the grief-stricken woman. Saw and could not hold herself back. She clipped the last pin on the clothes-line and abandoned the remaining wet clothes in the basket.

The black-skinned woman forced her heavy-set body into a brisk pace until she met the narrow road leading down the hill. She crossed the creek over a makeshift bridge and, breathing heavily, made her way along the thick foliage to where she supposed the woman to be.

The brush rustled and Margaret leaped up for fear that it was a wild animal or, even worse, some lewd man who spied her with the bodice of her dress open. The startled baby began wailing. Margaret flinched upon seeing a black face staring down at her. The woman held a hand to her chest trying to catch her breath. They silently stood eye to eye for a few moments until the black woman's breathing slowed. The stranger reached for Margaret's satchels and, before she could swat her arm away, the woman spoke.

"Come to the house an' get some tea an' a bite to eat."

Without any deliberation, the stranger walked away with her satchels in tow. Margaret found herself watching the backside of the heavy woman walking away from her. There was nothing left to do but comply. She roughly dried her eyes on her sleeves and followed the stranger.

At the top of the hill, they entered a yard with a small sign posted that read LAUNDRY FOR HIRE at the onset of the property. At the front door, they entered a room where a young black girl manned the front desk. Her air of importance changed to surprise as the elder woman led the white woman and infant to the part of the house reserved for liv-ing quarters. There she set the bags on the floor at the bottom of an open stairway.

"There's a empty cot in the room at the top of the stairs. Drop off yer satchels there, wash up, and I'll git a plate ready down here."

As if in a dream devoid of choices, Margaret ascended the stairs. She found a china washbasin and pitcher in the corner of the room and washed her face and hands with the cool water. She felt more human already. Maggie was fast asleep. Gently laying her on the cot and cover-ing her with a clean, thin flannel blanket, Margaret proceeded downstairs

Maggie's Way

to the parlor and dining room she had walked through earlier. She waited, aware of the young black girl who kept stealing glances at her when she thought Margaret was not watching. Soon, another woman old enough to be the child's mother was also peering around the corner.

The satchel-stealing woman returned with a plate of food as promised, along with a hot cup of tea. She motioned for Margaret to sit and vanished from the room. Margaret was not feeling hungry; she hadn't for days, but she sipped gratefully at the tea. She detected the scent of peppermint in the small, warm cloud of steam rising from the china cup. The woman returned with a cup of tea for herself, a bowl of sugar, and a fresh pitcher of cream.

"Eat while it's hot," the stranger prompted.

"I've not much of an appetite, but the tea is grand."

"Psshaw," the older woman said.

Margaret thought it aimed at her until she heard footsteps slide around the corner. Someone had been watching her again.

I must be quite the oddity, she thought.

"Ya best eat if ya don't want to lose your milk for yer young 'un."

How could she argue with that? Besides, it did seem ungrateful to refuse the stranger's hospitality. She began to eat.

"I'm Clara Brown, and who might ya be?" Her warm brown eyes penetrated Margaret's peaked face.

Margaret sensed a strong intelligence in those eyes.

"My name is Margaret O'Malley, and that's wee Maggie upstairs." As soon as she used Thomas's words, the tears came unbidden again.

Clara waited in silence for a few moments and then pulled up a chair next to the young white woman. She offered her a lace-edged handkerchief. It was so pretty that Margaret felt guilty soiling it, but with all this crying she needed a good nose blowing.

"So what troubles ya, child?"

UNLIKELY FRIENDSHIP

Margaret's Story

Thus began a friendship between the young Irish immigrant and the old freed slave woman. Strange as it seemed, it turned out they had a lot in common. Clara had arrived in June, only three months earlier than Margaret, and both had traveled the same westward trail in covered wagons. Both had worked as domestic help, except Clara performed without pay until she was able to purchase her freedom. Both had lost husbands. Twenty-two years earlier, Clara's husband and family vanished when the slave owner died and all the slaves were sold off. She had no idea where her family was or whether her husband was still alive.

Margaret found herself in awe of this woman who, after obtaining her freedom at the age of fifty-seven, headed West. This kind, diligent woman had the tenacity that was missing in many a much younger woman. Her example gave Margaret the courage and desire to go on with her life. She thanked heaven she still had her child. Disease could just as easily have taken her daughter. When Clara held Margaret against her heavy bosom in a comforting hug, it was the closest thing to her mother's love she had experienced in all the years she had been in America.

For the next year, Margaret lived with Clara, working in the laundry and cooking for the people living in the house, which varied at times from ten to fifteen people. Esther, the young girl with the curious eyes, often watched Maggie while Margaret worked; she turned out to be a very responsible and loving caregiver. In April 1860, the competing towns of Auraria and Denver City merged, and "Denver" became the community's official name.

Everyone who lived at Clara's home worked hard. None of them were strangers to hard work, and none forgot what Clara had done for them. Clara made good use of her freedom and became a successful businesswoman. Within five years, by 1864, she owned real estate in both Denver and Central City, a booming mining town in the nearby mountains.

Years later, Margaret told the story of the day a store clerk mistook Clara for Margaret's servant woman.

"You have clearly misunderstood, ma'am," Margaret said. "I work for this dear woman at her place of business."

Never in all her years had she seen such surprise on a woman's face. Shock transformed into disgust, and the clerk turned her back on both of them to wait on a more respectable woman. Margaret felt that the world had its head turned upside down when it came to who and what were truly valuable in this life.

FRESH START

In the spring of 1876, Ma and I headed out for the southwest part of the territory with Amos. Mrs. Jacobson thought Ma had lost her mind, leaving for the wilderness at her age, without a husband, and maybe even more scandalous, with a single man of "questionable virtue." I have to give Mrs. Jacobson credit, though, since she did acknowledge all those years of Ma's work with some bonus pay. Her son, Richard, also thought I was addled when I traded a braided leather halter for four pairs of his britches. I was not about to be tied down to dresses when I would be riding hundreds of miles. It was not too likely we would run into any proper ladies on our journey, anyway. Ma balked at first but soon came to appreciate my reasoning.

Amos grumbled for the first few days about the wisdom of bringing women along, but he finally reconciled himself to his decision. I think he was glad for the company but would never admit it, and, truth was, we were more dependable than strangers off the street. Ma drove the second supply wagon while I brought up the tail with the third wagon. Amos began to look quite the character after a few days of his beard growing out. The image of a clean-shaven shopkeeper was soon left behind in Denver. We discovered he was surely set in his ways and views on things, being a bachelor all those years. We just smiled and tolerated him. He certainly did grow to like Ma's cooking.

We set out south along the Front Range, using an old fur-trading route. Hitched behind my wagon was the new paint mare I had purchased with the money earned doing Henry's chores. Three teams of four mules each pulled the heavily loaded wagons. They contained the supplies that would line the shelves of Amos's general store at our destination in the San Juan Mountains, a place abounding with rumors of mineral riches. Uncompahgre City was the name of the new settlement.

After a few days, we turned west, our eyes directed to the foothills and, behind them, the stately Rocky Mountains. Suddenly, Amos's gravelly voice sang out — "I will lift up mine eyes unto the hills, from whence cometh my help. My help cometh from the Lord, which made heaven and earth."

That was when we knew Amos believed in the Almighty, too. If Ma harbored any hidden doubts about traveling with this man, I think she was reassured that day.

Throughout the foothills, we rode through squaw brush, rabbit brush, and sagebrush. The squaw brush bloomed cheerfully with light yellow flowers. Amos told us the shrub was also called "skunk brush," due to its strong smell. In contrast, the sagebrush smelled pleasant as I rolled it between my fingers, releasing its clean, sharp aroma. The gray-green leaves smelled faintly like the sage used in Ma's stuffing for birds.

Amos and I appreciated how Ma was up just before dawn, heating the water over a campfire. As a result, I enjoyed my first tin cup of coffee before I took the animals down to water in the morning. We started out early each day to avoid having to look for a campsite in the dark. Every five to seven days, I helped with the washing. Ma and I draped the dripping clothes over nearby trees or bushes in the late afternoon and allowed the hot sun to dry them.

Ma's delicious bread made it easier to down our daily meal of beans. Beans became a mainstay because dry beans never spoiled and, when cooked, were filling. Amos was always reminding us how many miles we needed to travel each day and discouraged Ma from taking too much time with the cooking. Ma had experience from years before with the problem of making bread while traveling. Bread dough rising in a deep kettle rested just behind the wagon seat during the midday heat. The close proximity made it handy for her to punch down the dough when it threatened to rise over the brim.

If Amos's aim was particularly good and luck (or Providence) provided a close shot at a deer or elk, we occasionally had the treat of freshly roasted meat. The leftovers would be dried into jerky. While watering the animals one day, I remembered Ma's canned raspberries. I had carefully packed two jars, despite Ma telling me it wasn't practical. The last time I had checked, the jars remained unbroken. I ran back, anticipating the considerable fortune of Ma baking one of her famous pies.

Amos walked up in the midst of our conversation. "We ain't got no time for bakin' if we're goin' to make any distance today." The furrows between his eyes deepened, as he meant to remind us who was in charge.

Ma put her hands to her waist and glared back at him. "Mr. Randall, I don't mean any disrespect, but we've been traveling for days and living off beans. I think it's about time we had a dessert."

I wondered who was going to back down first. A hawk cried overhead, the only sound breaking the silence of that uncomfortable moment. At last,

Amos threw his hat down on the ground. "Make your darn pie, but don't let this be a reg'lar event." He picked up his hat, shook the dust from it, and sauntered off. I heard him mumbling something about darn, troublesome women. I looked over at Ma, who was smiling in victory like it was Judgment Day and Jesus, himself, was standing there with open arms.

That evening, it was downright humorous to watch Amos dig into his piece of that disputed pie. When he finished, he wiped the crumbs from his moustache and cleared his throat. I watched as his eyes moved around the campsite, returning to the tin of pie on the back plank of the wagon where Ma set the food.

"Amos," Ma said softly, "can I talk you into another piece of pie?" A coy smile played over her face.

"Yes, Ma'am," he said. He watched as she slowly placed the pie on his plate, his eyes averted from her face.

"Good pie, Ma'am," he said. He walked over to a nearby rock and sat down with his back to us.

I broke out laughing then, despite Ma's repeated admonitions. When she saw I was not going to stop any time soon, she gave up and laughed with me. Amos turned around and to our surprise, he was grinning too.

One morning, I asked Amos how he knew how many miles we had traveled each day.

"I look out 'cross the horizon 'n locate a landmark di'rectly ahead on our route." He spoke with an air of importance as our sole guide and leader. "I eyeball the length, figur' the distance, and start all o'er again."

Risking that he might take my request as lack of faith in his ability, I asked for a mile estimation out of curiosity. Since I had often ridden the Jacobson's horses down the two-mile lane, I figured I had a fair idea of what constituted a mile on horseback. I soon agreed; Amos knew his mileage.

Each evening after dinner, Amos unrolled his survey map of the central and southern Rockies territory and studied it. By the time Ma and I had finished the dishes and general cleaning up, he would be ready to show us the next day's route. Amos always complimented Ma's cooking, even when the menu varied little from day to day. I think he was becoming sweet on my mother, but I didn't see it having any effect on her. She appreciated Amos as a good and God-fearing man, but that was as far as it went as near as I could tell. I was enjoying Amos's company since I had never known my father, or any grown man for that matter — other than Henry. He was becoming a good friend, how I supposed an uncle might be.

I asked once why Amos chose mules to haul the wagons.

"I can sell 'em for a profit at the mines," he explained. "'cause miners use 'em for haulin'."

Amos felt the mule was a better choice over a horse anyway, for it took on the best qualities of both an ass and a horse, of which the mule was the offspring. The mule retained the surefootedness and endurance of the donkey, along with the spirit and energy of the horse. I learned over the span of the journey that a mule will not overeat like a horse, which would literally eat oats until it killed itself.

The landscape varied tremendously as we traveled. At times, the pines enveloped the hillsides; at other times, quaking aspen covered the slopes. Open valleys alternated with close trails through thick forests. One day, Amos motioned to me, his head nodding toward a distant hill where several Ute Indians solemnly surveyed our passage.

ROLLS OF THUNDER

Ma had not noticed the natives, and I decided it wise to keep quiet unless it proved necessary to let her know. It was a chilling experience for the next few hours. Although days earlier Amos spoke about the relative peaceful behavior of the natives, I also knew enough to realize we were passing through their country. Certainly, any people would resent invaders. The day proved uneventful, but, as with an unspoken agreement, Amos and I did not speak about the incident in Ma's presence for a few days. When we did, she related her experiences moving out West years ago. Here I was trying to protect a woman who had faced her own risks and adventures.

Gray clouds coagulated in the morning and by noon enveloped the sky. We were nearing Cochetopa Pass, where a steep hill hindered our travel. Halfway up the hill and after several tries, it became evident that the mules could not haul the heavily loaded wagons up the slope. Amos directed us to unload the first wagon. It seemed like too much trouble, but Amos assured us it was the only way to get our wagons up.

Amos staked the empty wagon on the hilltop. The belly of the wagon was propped up to make the rear set of wheels run free. We tied the front wheels with thick rope to the upper part of the wagon to keep them immobile. Amos secured a strong rope to the axle. He threw me the other end of the long rope and directed me to pull it down to the second wagon, which remained stocked with supplies. There he joined me and tied the end of the rope to the front axle. Ma, Amos, and I trudged back to the top of the hill. Amos unhitched the mules from the first wagon and tied two mules, one each, to a back spoke on the rear wheels. Amos stationed himself beside the left rear wagon wheel, while Ma and I waited by the right.

Amos yelled at the mules, whipping them forward. We pushed the wheels, our hands gripping the spokes. Our combined effort tediously reeled the wagon uphill.

Frequently, the mules were stopped, and the rope retied on different spokes on the revolving wheels. I looked at Ma, whose brows knit together. She looked at me for a moment, and unspoken concern passed between us. After an hour, the second wagon was at the top. The procedure was repeated. The last wagon was nearly to the top when it caught in a small depression in the ground. Amos went to the unmoving wheel, braced himself, and pulled the wheel upwards.

"Go!" he yelled. Ma and I prodded the mules on as Amos pulled on the spokes of the offending wheel. The wagon lurched, and the wheels spun again.

"Hurrah!" I yelled. All the wagons were at the top. A moment after my display of exuberance, I saw Amos fall to the ground, the reward of his mighty effort. I laughed heartily until I observed he was not getting up, not even moving.

Ma and I reached him almost simultaneously. Ma reached out her hand to find the pulse in his wrist beating strong. He remained still. She gingerly lifted his head to discover a crimson stained rock, still warm and wet. A fleeting look of total helplessness passed over her face. The moment passed.

"Get a dishtowel, Maggie," she said, "and grab the folded canvas in the back of the second wagon."

"Now!" she yelled, when she saw I still stood there staring at Amos.

I ran, gathered the items, and raced back. My mother's lips moved in silent words. They ceased when I arrived, and she proceeded to wrap the towel around Amos's head. Then she laid the canvas on the ground next to him.

"Maggie, take his arm and leg on your side," she said. She picked up his other arm and leg. "We're going to move him onto the canvas." Her eyes bored into mine. "Carefully."

We moved Amos's still figure onto the canvas. We lifted him barely above the ground and moved him closer to the wagons.

"We're camping here," Ma said. "Maggie, gather firewood."

I prayed while I gathered wood. The sky darkened earlier than usual with heavy, threatening clouds. A sickening sensation pulled in my stomach. We were nearly halfway on our journey — too far to go back, too many miles yet to go. What would happen to us if Amos died?

When I returned to the wagons with an armload of wood, Ma was leaning over Amos. He was softly groaning.

"Amos, we need to get you in the wagon. Grab his other arm, Maggie. Amos, help us get you in the wagon."

Another groan came as Amos slowly raised his head. He managed to sit up. With all our strength, Ma and I lifted him to his feet. Thankfully, Amos had a slight build. Shortly after he was in the wagon, he passed out again. Ma cushioned his bandaged head with a down-filled pillow and covered him with a quilt. This done, I went for more wood. Ma started the dinner while I secured the animals.

The beans were only lukewarm when the thunder arrived. High in the mountains, thunder reverberates as loud as exploding dynamite. With a cloth in her hand, Ma grabbed the kettle and carried it into the wagon where Amos was still unconscious. The rain came heavy like the wrath of God. We ate by candlelight as the rain beat on the canvas, thrusting it back and forth in the wind. Ma's face was solemn, and she stared at her plate, making no attempt at conversation. This was all my fault. I had brought this on us with my fearless dreams of adventure. How could I have done this to her?

I wanted to cry, to say how sorry I was, but under the circumstances I knew I needed to be strong. Whatever came, we would need two strong heads to deal with it. I prayed for God's merciful protection.

Amos fell in and out of consciousness for two days. During that time, Ma told me about her journey West with my father. When she came to the part about father's death, she wept — the only time I saw my mother cry. Then I recognized the solemn looks that had passed over her face in the last few days. Amos's accident had triggered too many memories and fears.

"Ma," I said, "do you regret making this trip?"

Her high cheekbones rose, her smile lighting her face. "No, dear one." She placed her hand over mine. "Life is too short to waste on regrets."

Amos came round on the third day. It seemed symbolic of another resurrection. Ma insisted on a fourth day of ease to ensure his full recovery.

"Aw, women," he grumbled, "always slowin' ya down."

We laughed. That was when we knew Amos was going to be all right.

13

WESTWARD JOURNEY

A few days west of Cochetopa Pass, Ma, Amos, and I spotted our first prospector. We had crossed paths with a few before but always from a distance. Their worn, dirty attire might vary, but the fiercely independent countenance was recognizably the same. Their mules or donkeys were always loaded down with picks, shovels, and jacks, along with meager provisions for survival. A rifle packed by a prospector's side provided occasional game meat and self-protection, if needed. His nomadic way of life called for nature's ever-available accommodations: a fallen log for a chair, a rock overhang or thick trees for a shelter, and a flat rock for a makeshift table.

We came across Johann one day as he knelt at a stream we were soon to cross. He looked up, perturbed that we had interrupted his activity: panning for gold. I noticed his hand crept to the pistol hidden just inside his tattered, dirty coat, but when he saw we were two women and a man, he relaxed. His wariness dissolved as he talked to Amos. His scraggly beard covered his face, but there was no hiding the German accent in his English. With the unkempt manner, I could not tell if he was any younger than Amos, who was quite scruffy himself by now. He camped with us that night and shared his remaining sourdough bread. It had an unusual but tasty flavor. He explained to Ma how the starter mixture could be kept endlessly, eliminating the need for purchasing yeast. After our evening meal, I noticed he walked to his packs and retrieved a bottle of some kind of liquor. After several swigs, he returned to the campfire. I figured not to say anything to Amos unless it got out of hand. Amos did not believe in partaking of any spirits. I took note as Johann talked about the different aspects of prospecting. He pursued placer mining by panning for traces of gold in a stream; at other times, he would check an open cut to investigate the soil just above bedrock. Sometimes, he explained, he would sink a small shaft to further examine the rock below the ground.

Johann told us quite the tales by the campfire.

"One ol' prospector," Johann began, "came 'pon a streak o' gold on the side o' a hill. Well, that ol' lucky fella begin to folla that streak. It went on and on. After two days of followin' that golden thread, he discovered the biggest gold-bearin' quartz mine in Nevada." In another tale, he told one story about a prospector finding a nugget as big as his fist. Several stories he told (with slight variants) were of prospectors who sold their claims for thousands of dollars to capitalists back East.

I realized these tales were a combination of rumor, exaggeration, and speculation, but to every tale there is an element of truth. My stomach leaped with the excitement and adventure of the place we were soon to experience. The next morning I ventured to ask Johann to show me how he panned for gold. He was amazed at why a young woman would need to know such things. He studied me for a moment and shook his head at my strange attire of men's trousers, but then proceeded to demonstrate the technique. His comment was meant to admonish me to stick to my dresses and housework but, perhaps out of thankfulness for our food and company, he granted my request. He took his old cast-iron pan from his ass's pack, and I followed him down to the creek. I knew I would have to be attentive, because I suspected he was not going to do much explaining.

He scooped up the gravel from the bottom of the river while he stood midway across the stream. He walked back to where I stood at the edge. The creek water filled near to the top of the pan, brown and cloudy from the dirt and sand floating in the disturbed water. Johann tipped the pan and allowed some of the water to spill. He sloshed the water to the right and left and back again, each time releasing a slight amount of the water.

"Color is heavier," he spoke at last, referring to the gold itself. Fine-grained black sand remained in the pan. He moved the pan toward me.

"Look," he commanded.

I peered into the pan, seeing only fine gravel and shook my head puzzled.

"See!"

I looked again trying to scrutinize the contents. I didn't see a fist-sized nugget or, for that matter, even a tooth-sized one.

A grumble in his throat rose, as his mouth turned down. Johann dipped a thick finger onto the sand. He turned it over in front of my face. At last I saw the fine gold flake gleaming, tiny though it was.

"Gold!" I exclaimed.

I looked further into the pan and saw four or five other miniscule pieces of gold. Johann took a small glass vial out of his pocket and placed the small flakes into the water-filled container. He motioned me to place the other grains into the vial. When I was finished, he put the cork stopper into place and handed it to me.

Maggie's Way

"For me?"

He nodded. He smiled patronizingly as if giving a child a souvenir of something that was beyond her future experiences. He returned to his ass and replaced the iron skittle in his panniers. He gestured goodbye to all, and we watched as he rode off into the depths of the mountains, following no path save his own sense of future discoveries and riches.

14

NEARING THE SAN JUANS

Traveling across the Rocky Mountains drew new vistas with each passing day. Many of the peaks exceeded ten thousand feet, the highest fourteen thousand or more. Streams surged down rocky slopes as the snowpack melted. They filled numerous lakes, only to run off and rush eastward toward the Gulf of Mexico or westward into the Colorado River and eventually into the Gulf of California. The water's flow depended on which side of the Continental Divide the streams happened to be located. Many beautiful waterfalls came into view as we continued on our journey at higher elevations. Amos, who had studied the geology of the range, informed us of the volcanic activity and glaciers that had formed the mountains long ago. Inspired by the scenery, I had come up with a proper name, at last, for my horse. My mare's name became "Sierra," Spanish for "mountain range."

We were steadily making progress westward. It was a damp, dreary day when we rode through Gunnison, the drizzle pressing close to snow with the temperature near freezing at that high altitude. It was not much of a town: the main dirt road through the little habitation revealed log shacks with a few crude frame houses. We passed by one of these houses that was recently boarded up. A man wearing a long, heavy wool coat stood on the small porch nailing a notice on the front door. Amos had slowed to a weary pace moving through the town, so it was quite easy for me to bring my team to a halt. Ma always said I was more curious than a cat. From where I sat on the wagon seat, I could read the lettering. In large bold print it read:

CHURCH CLOSED. GOD IS MOVING TO UNCOMPAHGRE CITY.

After finishing his posting, the man became aware of my presence. He looked like any in these parts: heavily bearded, worn clothing exposed beneath the unbuttoned overcoat. He appeared young enough around the eyes. Not as young as me, but compared to Amos, a much younger man. Without intending to, I found myself announcing to him that

Uncompahgre City was our destination also. (Perhaps the expectant way he stared prompted me to speak to the stranger.) Upon my abrupt declaration, his mouth turned up into a gracious and, I might add, humored smile. I prodded my team to catch up with the rest, regretting I had allowed myself to become sidetracked.

On the next day, we descended in elevation, and the wind turned to a warmer current. We passed through deep ravines in which the Gunnison River flowed. The landscape transformed into an arid region with blue-gray sage replacing the alpine trees. Eventually, the mountains receded into the distance, giving way to hills. This was mesa country. Eroded buttes arose in varied earth colors of vivid sienna, ochre, and umber while the sage and rabbit brush were constant companions to the scenery. We continued through such country for several days. Although it had a strange beauty, I found myself yearning for a return to mountain country.

One day, while moving through this landscape, a lone rider on a smart black steed came up behind us. He slowed as he drew up to where I sat on the wagon seat. He tipped his hat and chuckled as he saw my surprise. I gasped; it was the man who had posted the sign on the building. My face burned hot as he caught up to Amos and rode alongside him for a while, intent in conversation. At last, he spurred his mount into an easy lope and easily distanced himself from us. My curiosity burned the rest of the day, knowing I could not question Amos until we stopped to make camp for the evening. At last, the day's travel came to an end. While Ma finished up with our evening meal, I questioned Amos about the man.

"That fellow's a man of God, a travelin' preacher. Can you believe it? A nice chap headed for Uncompahgre City. It appears a bit of civilization precedes us, ladies."

"A preacher?" I declared.

Amos looked at me as if I was fringing on blasphemy.

"Somehow, he doesn't fit the part." I said.

"You are no longer in Denver City, Maggie," Ma said. "We should be happy enough there will be a preacher in this remote settlement. The Lord knows a fresh mining town will need more than a bit of taming."

I felt properly chastened and kept my opinions to myself. Amos then declared that we were closing in at last to our destination, no more than four days. His thick hand pointed in the distance, where we could see rugged snow-capped mountains. Although a long way off, it was exciting to think our new home lay beneath those magnificent peaks.

On this last leg of our journey, sighting other travelers was an infrequent occurrence. Once we met up with a small group of cowpunchers and a blacksmith hired by the agent at the Ute Indian Agency, a site we would eventually pass as we neared our destination. Occasionally, we came upon a miner. The closer we came to Uncompahgre City, the more apparent it became that prospectors were headed there too.

I grew more excited as each hour drew us nearer to the new mining town. Finally came the day, April 26 to be exact, that we rounded a high hill where the Uncompahgre River lay below. We were greeted with a breathtaking sight: the San Juan Mountains loomed high above, rising in all their grandeur. I counted eight mountain peaks: four on each side, forming an amphitheater. Each mountain slope graduated back one upon another, as the center peaks formed the back part of the Uncompahgre bowl, where the fledgling town lay yet unseen. Uncompahgre City was still an hour's ride ahead, but I could tolerate it, knowing it was the end of our journey. Along the way, we witnessed prospectors panning for gold in the river.

We followed the Uncompahgre as it curved through the narrowing landscape, forested hills rising high on each side of us. At last, the land opened up to reveal a dramatic sight: the Uncompahgre Bowl with its towering peaks. Steep, rugged hills ascended on all sides with colors of sienna, gold, umber, and violet painted on nature's magnificent canvas. I was blind to the trail ahead of me as I took in the amazing sights high above. I saw several discovery cuts high on the mountainsides, a few so fresh I caught sight of the prospectors responsible. The bowl itself was quite barren looking, with frequent stumps in evidence of a once-forested area. Frontiersmen slashed all the trees for the express purpose of building the scattered shacks and log cabins seen in the distance.

Ma cajoled me into changing into a dress for our arrival to the settlement. It hardly made any difference; it was not much of a town. Isolated frame buildings made up the small, sparse business district, and the "streets" were rough dirt roads with deep ruts. We soon discovered that the name of the town had changed during the winter. It was now called "Ouray" after the Ute chief from that area.

Amos wasted no time in inquiring about a place to set up shop. Ma and I sat together on one of the wagons and watched a man hang a sign on a newly constructed blacksmith shop. The men walking back and forth among the businesses were a motley bunch. Most were unwashed and unshaven, and many had tattered clothing. I saw two men in fringed buckskin. I doubted they had come to be miners; more likely they were hunters or traders. I didn't see a reason to dress like a proper lady here. I had become quite comfortable in trousers and would not give them up. Ma would just have to live with it, I reasoned.

Maggie's Way

Within an hour and a half, Amos returned and directed Ma and me around to the rear of a building. Having been in town not quite two hours, we were helping Amos unpack his supplies. A businessman was renting out half of his building. After the rough winter they had experienced, he was more than accommodating to Amos, who had arrived with fresh staples. It turned out the roads had often been impassable, and food supplies had dwindled to the point of dining on bread and coffee. Many of the prospectors killed cattle belonging to the Ute Indian Agency, and others feared starvation before the first supplies could arrive. Amos was the second food supplier to show up this spring, and already he had an eager clientele.

Amos offered us temporary wages to help get his business up and running. We would all three board above the store on the second floor. Part of my wages went to boarding my horse at a nearby stable. We worked late into the night, along with the owner of the building, Mr. McCall, who volunteered to help. Amos unloaded all supplies for fear of theft from the eager bystanders, who watched us as if we were a gift from God himself. I suppose, in fact, Amos's supplies were.

After a very short night of sleep with a blanket hung as a divider between our bedding areas, we opened at nine o'clock. A crowd had gathered by eight o'clock that morning. Although the assembly consisted mainly of men, Ma and I waited on a half-dozen women who were a combination of businessmen's wives, saloon girls, and one scraggly prospector's wife. That is, I thought her scraggly until I picked up a looking glass for sale and saw my own wanting appearance. My unwashed hair appeared determined to escape the confines of a hastily arranged braiding.

It turned out the local businessmen were a tight lot, and a local assayer agreed to give assessment on nuggets of gold — a common currency in the mining town. After we closed at seven-thirty that evening, Amos was out making arrangements for a new shipment of supplies, which would arrive in four weeks. He already talked about stockpiling for next winter and making allowance for the mining rush. The increasing flow of men into the area kept pace with the spread of news that riches were indeed to be found here.

Before I realized it, three weeks had passed. How time had disappeared! Owing to our perseverance and hard work, customers found merchandise neatly stacked on shelves. One morning I overheard Amos suggesting that he could use Ma's help long term at the store. Two customers walked in about that time, diverting her attention. Later, I asked her outright whether she was thinking of taking Amos up on his offer.

"I believe I'll go into business for myself," was her reply.

Ouray, Colorado. From a Photograph by W. H. Jackson & Co., Denver. Supplement to *Harper's Weekly*, June 8, 1899

15

ENTREPRENEURS AND UNCONVENTIONAL LADIES

This news was an unexpected turn of events. Ma explained that a small frame building at the end of the street was up for lease; the man who had run a leather business had decided to work one of his mining prospects full time. Her intention was to open a restaurant.

"It will be much harder than working for Amos," I replied.

"It's what I best know how to do. Furthermore, all my life I have worked for others, and for once, I want to answer only to myself."

I was proud of my mother. I also knew by her decision that she saw no future with Amos and viewed him merely as a friend. I believe she also knew that working for him, while knowing how he felt, would be unkind. My mother was no stranger to hard work, and I applauded her endeavor to be a businesswoman.

Apparently, Ma's mind had whirled for some time over this new venture. This was evident in the way she rapidly organized her restaurant. There were few pauses to consider where or how she wanted things organized; she already had it figured. She might have waited months for a cast-iron cookstove to be shipped, but Amos, the dear, sold his to Ma in exchange for one free meal a day. He had become accustomed to her cooking and had found a way, short of marriage, to continue the benefits.

I helped Ma sew curtains for the restaurant windows. The red calico print material had come from Amos's stock, but this and everything else she paid for with the money earned setting up his store. The curtains produced cheer and warmth to the otherwise monotonous wooden walls. With part of her savings gleaned from over the years, Ma purchased a high-back sofa, an oak rocker, and an oval dining table with chairs for a private parlor in the back of the building. The high-quality furniture came from a businessman's wife who decided it was better to have a long-distance marriage than to live in the wilderness. Ma was quite determined in her plans and had the landlord, Mr. Hall, build a partition dividing the kitchen from her sitting room. He must have felt she was a good business risk because she got him to add on an open porch back there, too.

Ma and I slept up above the new restaurant. Mr. Hall put up a wall to make two bedrooms for us. I had never seen Ma so determined, and more surprising was the way she managed to acquire what she wanted. She found a furniture maker to build tables and chairs for the restaurant. They were on the simple side, but efficient for the purpose. Jud Abercomby was a friendly sort and worked long hours to get the furniture finished within a month. He was a tall man, rather overweight, with bright ruddy cheeks regardless of the weather. His breath always carried a hint of mint. As I was soon to discover, people in these rough mining towns were full of contrasts and contradictions. It turned out Jud Abercomby was also Reverend Abercomby from St. Louis. He was an agreeable person, always acknowledging me when I entered the room. Soon he had talked Ma into allowing him to lease the room on Sunday mornings for a small percentage of the collection plate. Once a week, the tables were stacked against one end of the room, and the chairs were laid out in straight rows. I went to his services more than once, and the message pretty much followed the Scriptures, as far as I could tell.

Business did not need to be drummed up in a frontier town such as this. People needed to eat, especially hard-driving prospectors and miners. Ma and I labored preparing the food each evening and morning, along with the continual chore of cleaning up. This certainly was not my intention for moving here. Soon, I was itching to get outdoors and explore the area. Throwing the dishwater out back one morning, my eyes longingly reached for the mountains. The air was fresh, and the clear sky promised a fine day. If I could only saddle my horse and ride today . . .. Clanging pots rang out in the kitchen. I sighed, took a deep breath, and trudged back inside to help Ma with the chores.

Mr. Miller, the blacksmith, often ate at our restaurant and had unknowingly tipped me off a few days ago about Dunnick's hiring on a few stable boys. Amos put a good word in for me, as he knew the owner from selling his mules there. I had obtained a job working with the horses.

Ma was quite settled now into her daily routine of work. I took a deep breath and approached her later that morning.

"Ma, Cara Johnson was asking about hiring on with us." Truth was, I had approached the girl about the subject. She was the blacksmith's daughter.

"She seems like a responsible girl, and I do need to replace you," Ma said. Her back was to me as washed the everlasting dishes. When she found me speechless, she turned to meet my eyes.

Maggie's Way

"You *do* have something lined up by now, don't you, Maggie?"

"Yes, Ma, I do." I smiled. The dawn was breaking through a long night.

The next morning, I rose while it was yet dark. I wound my hair into one single braid at the back of my neck. I slipped my legs once again into the faded black trousers and canvas shirt. I grabbed the broad-brimmed hat that I had worn as protection against the sun and the wind on our long journey from Denver. Without waking Ma, I crept down to the kitchen and started a fire in the cookstove for making my breakfast. I stood shivering in front of the stove, trying to absorb the heat until the room warmed.

After a hearty breakfast of slapjacks, bacon, and fried potatoes, I left the coffee simmering for Ma. I stepped out the back door and walked around to the main road that ran through the business section of town. The light was beginning its journey behind the mountain walls that surrounded Ouray. The valley and all the town buildings remained in shadow, waiting for the sun to clear the peaks. I tucked my braid beneath my broad-brimmed hat as I watched the clear morning light hit the highest rocky peaks above. The first rays of dawn reflected rose and violet hues over the clouds.

I walked through the eerie stillness of the streets; the businesses would not open for two hours. Down a side street, I saw a prospector leading his packed mule, heading out for the day. In less than a quarter of a mile, I reached my destination. Next to the blacksmith's shop stood a long narrow barn with a crudely carved wooden sign in front which announced: DUN-NICK'S FREIGHTING. I pulled half of the double barn doors open, just far enough to slide in and close the heavy door behind me.

"Over here, boy," a loud, coarse voice called. My eyes had not adjusted to the dark interior of the building, so I walked toward the general vicinity of the sound. I figured I was more than likely the "boy" the voice was speaking to.

"Ya can start by forkin' fresh hay to each horse's stall."

I flinched at the loud voice, which bellowed nearer than I expected. My eyes focused just as a big black man shoved a pitchfork at me. A couple of seconds slower and I may have had the handle shoved into my jaw.

"Name's Jonas. Now git to work, boy." He walked back toward the middle of the long, extended building.

I said nothing.

The sound of hooves moving in anticipation of their morning feeding filled me with delight. I drew in the smells of the place: the aroma of warm animal flesh — mules and horses — and fresh hay. I rubbed the velvet noses, filled the troughs with hay, then mucked out their stalls.

Later Jonas returned, as I was finishing.

"Over there's the horses," he said. " Brush 'em down an' check their hooves. Make sure ya do an extra good job of groomin' the bay geldin' in the first stall an' the gray mare next to 'im. Mrs. Hanson an' her daughter ride 'em. We don't want no accidents 'cause ya forgot to get the burrs under the belly, now."

I waited uncomfortably for him to realize he'd mistaken me for a boy, but he never looked at me closely.

Two hours later, Mr. Dunnick came in, marching straight up to me. He was a coarse man as many were here, cussing every other word. He was over six feet tall with a beard that was showing streaks of gray; his body was muscled from working as a farrier most of his life.

"Now I am going to be damn honest with you, Miss. I have serious doubts about a gal working here, but Amos has been good with credit for me at his store, so I am damn well going to try to return the favor. He says you have a way with animals, but that doesn't mean a damn diddly if you are afraid of hard work. So you are fair warned, I'd say. Jonas, come over here."

Jonas dropped a burlap sack of oats against a wooden stall and walked over.

"How's she been working out? I want the truth now, no protecting her because she's a gal."

Jonas's eyes stared at me as if one of the horses had spoken or a cow had jumped over the moon. The look vanished, and he answered, "I ain't seen no slackin' so far, sir. Worked hard an' constant."

"Let's hope she keeps it up, then." Dunnick said, looking straight at me. Then he walked to the front of the barn where a small office had been walled in on one side.

"Don't forget about the dozen mules scheduled for ten o'clock, Jonas."

"Yessir."

I looked at Jonas and saw him scrutinizing me.

"Are ya that gal at the restaurant? Margaret's daughter?"

"Yes, sir."

"Well, I can see yar not afraid of hard work, but bes' keep on yar toes."

His eyes softened then, and he warned me that Dunnick was a hard taskmaster, not standing for any foolery or laziness.

"Why ya ain't preferrin' to help yar mother is one on me, Miss."

Maggie's Way

"Call me Maggie, sir. I have always preferred working with animals to cooking any day."

Jonas walked away shaking his head, but not before I caught a glimpse of a grin.

Burros packed for the mountains —
a street scene in Ouray.
Harper's Weekly 1893

16

HOUSE OF THE SAINTS

After one of the stable hands quit, I began working full time. Dunnick's carried out brisk trade as throngs of prospectors swept into the Ouray bowl and hundreds of claims went on file. New mining sites needed timber and tools while the miners required food supplies to hold them at least a week until they returned to town. Since most of the mineral finds were located high above in these rugged mountains, donkeys or mules were required to transport heavy equipment and ore up and down the mountainsides. I watched the men pack the animals with supplies. The mules were tied together single file, sometimes up to sixteen mules in a pack train. Jonas told me a mule could carry three-hundred-and-fifty pounds of ore. He soon had me try my hand at fitting a mule with the wooden cross saddle over a saddle pad. He showed me how to constrict the cinch to prevent the pack from slipping. I thought him cruel for causing so much discomfort to the poor animal until he explained a loose pack would harm the mule's back.

Two hours after the packer had arrived for his mule train, I watched them file down the road loaded with food supplies, some with long pieces of lumber trailing in the dirt, and one unfortunate animal loaded with a heavy cast-iron pot belly stove. It was a miserable life for these animals as they struggled daily with heavy burdens. Their only reprieve was at night when their packs were unloaded and their food supplied.

I was glad to exercise the horses on those rare days when there were no requests for them. They were fortunate in that they had reprieves from duty and did not carry heavy loads. Later, I was to see they did not escape abuse altogether, such as when they had been ridden too hard and too long with little food or water.

At first, when I walked back and forth to work, people overlooked me as a young lad and not much notice was given. However, when the word got out among the businessmen's families, I attracted much attention among the wives and daughters. In the beginning, it was just whispering behind a hand, and then it was holding their skirts to one side as if my unacceptability might rub off on them. After a while, I steered clear of walking on the side of the street where any of these "respectable" ladies walked, but it was not always avoidable since they could appear from a doorway at any moment.

In contrast, I did not experience this treatment from wives of craftsmen or miners. A friendly offer of help from a poor working-class person is far sweeter than approval from a rich man, who deems himself better than the rest of humanity due to the sheer size of his bank account. I did not reveal any of this to Ma because I did not want her to worry, along with the fact that I was not about to change my ways anytime soon.

I had been working at Dunnick's for about three weeks when one of the geldings boiled over. One of the lads had just saddled him and was aiming to warm the horse up by riding him back and forth in front of the stables. The horse threw a royal fit. It was a sight to see: ears laid back, snorting, bucking . . . soon the lad kissed the ground. At that point, I hurried over to grab the horse's reins to save the men the trouble of chasing a runaway. I slowly walked up to the horse, whispered to him, and reminded him it was I who groomed, fed, and watered him after a long day of riding. He was breathing hard, but his ears were no longer laid back. I knew he was no danger to me.

I don't know why I decided to climb in the saddle other than to teach this horse not to fear a rider. He watched me warily with the whites of his eyes showing, but when I calmly sat there and gave no commands, just patted and talked to him, he relaxed. Then I nudged him forward, sauntered him down the street, and turned around. There was Mr. Dunnick, standing with his hands on his hips, staring. I feared I had been out of order. I dismounted then in front of him and began to explain myself.

A burst of applause rose from the small crowd that had gathered, along with a few hoots and hollers and a whistle. My eyes caught sight of the face of the lad who had been thrown: red and contorted in anger at being shown up by a girl. He spun around and stomped off.

"Good job, Miss," Dunnick announced. "You are permanently on the payroll, with a raise to commence next pay day." He tramped back to the stable.

Then Jonas and a couple of stable lads slapped me on the back before we all went back to work. I believe it was from that day on that the other lads accepted me there. I had proven myself.

Later that evening, Ma asked me to accompany her to a church service the following morning at a different locale.

"Where will it be?" I asked.

"Wait until morning," she answered with a twinkle in her eyes.

The next morning, I dressed in proper clothes for the first time in weeks, my hair done up for the service. As we walked down Main Street for a couple of blocks, our high-buttoned shoes hammered over the boardwalk, announcing our progress. Others were similarly attired and arriving from various directions. Soon Ma stopped in front of a building with a large carved sign announcing the Bucket of Blood Saloon.

I was indeed amazed as I followed her through the swinging doors: of all places, a drinking establishment. Wide-eyed, I took in the building. Beer kegs sat in orderly rows in the back where they had run out of the bentwood chairs used at gambling tables: latecomers would have to sit on these. A white cloth was draped over a large painting behind the bar. I had heard about these paintings through the old women's hen scratching at the restaurant. They were usually nude pictures of questionable ladies. The massive oak bar that served distilled spirits to hundreds of men was now an altar, a large cross of sanded planks taking main stage. We had arrived early enough to sit in the chairs three rows toward the front.

"You can close your mouth now, Maggie dear," Ma whispered.

I pondered the irony of the righteous gathering where the unsaved had been booze blinded the night before, but, at last, I appreciated the contradiction and smiled. The chairs soon filled up, and someone in the back played a violin rendition of "Amazing Grace" to start out the service. We all knew this song by heart, and a hearty chorus rang out. When the song ended, the minister walked up to the makeshift altar. What a Judgment Day surprise I felt when the clergyman turned to face the eager congregation. Expecting the rotund face and figure of Reverend Abercomby, I was surprised to see the trim figure of a much younger man. The preacher's eyes caught mine at that moment, and the man smiled at me. He was clean-cut and sensible looking. Then I gasped. I recognized the mocking twinkle in those blue eyes — the man from Gunnison who had passed us on our journey to Ouray! The beard had been trimmed, revealing an unfamiliar face, but it was definitely him. I sneaked a peak at Ma, but she just looked straight ahead, smiling all the same. He addressed the congregation and introduced himself as Reverend Matthew Harding.

The sermon became just a bit too long for my likes, and I fought the overpowering urge to yawn. About that time, his voice took on a different quality with more urgency, more inflection — could I even say excitement? He spoke about the fact that we were all pilgrims in this new community, having ventured to the unknown, hoping for new and better opportunities. He talked about having faith in the Creator who had made this panorama of beauty and splendor around us, and how He would not forsake us as long as we looked to Him in everything. I began to have a better opinion of the man, never having heard any minister sermonize like that.

I found myself waiting, expecting a climax to his sermon. Jalapeño peppers! I was not disappointed.

" . . . and just as our Savior spent a bucket of blood for our salvation . . ."

I looked around at all the faces held with rapt attention, not even blinking at the crude reference to the name of the establishment. Was I the only one who felt it was irreverent? Blazes! I couldn't help it; I began to smile and, ultimately, to laugh inwardly. I am sure the row of parishioners behind me thought I was moved to tears, but, the truth was, I was in much discomfort from the effort of keeping silent. An elbow dug into my side, and Ma reminded me to behave myself. However, the restrained laughter would start up again, and I would get another jab. Luckily, the Reverend had ended his sermon and was moving down the middle of the rows of saloon chairs to greet people as they left. Noise from all the people visiting and moving about permitted me to laugh at last.

"Maggie, girl, what am I going to do with you?" Ma said. Soon, she was joining me in laughter.

"All right, let us compose ourselves so we can greet Reverend Harding and go home."

I kept my composure as we neared the preacher in the greeting line. At last, it was our turn, and Ma thanked him for the good message and gave him an invitation to her restaurant for a free cup of coffee and dessert any time. Then it was my turn to extend my hand in greeting.

"That was quite a show you put on yesterday at Dunnick's." His eyes twinkled when he saw my surprise that he had witnessed the scene. "You're quite the horsewoman."

I felt my cheeks grow warm.

"I am so glad that my message appeared to hit home with you."

With a tilt of my chin, I met his gaze and smiled.

"I found your message very refreshing and . . . original." I accentuated my words and looked up at him. *Highly unorthodox, but original.*

"Quite a compliment coming from a lady such as yourself, I am sure."

"Good day, Sir." I was vexed at his barbed remark, directed, surely, at my occupation.

"Good day to you, ladies."

"By the way," his voice followed us.

Ma and I turned around.

"I'll take you up on your offer, Mrs. O'Malley, for that pie and coffee."

He glanced at Ma and then smiled at me. I blushed again, a curse of my fair skin. As soon as we were out of earshot, I asked Ma why she had ever offered such an invitation.

"Why, Maggie, I was only being polite. He seems like a nice man. Is something troubling you, dear?"

"Of course not, Ma."

17

SILVER IN THOSE HILLS

That very afternoon following the unusual church service, I vowed to take a decent ride at last. With all the busyness since arriving in Ouray, I had found little time to ride my horse. Amos insisted that I take a rifle. With the mountains filled with prospectors ready to fight for their claims, not to mention Indians lurking in the hills, one could not be too careful. I borrowed his rifle without admitting that I didn't know how to use it.

I crossed the Uncompahgre River and headed up a narrow deer trail that switchbacked up the steep mountainside like a side-winding snake, twisting ever higher. The sweet, fresh scent of pine drifted through the forested hills. Colorful flowers sprung up on the open ground beneath the forest canopy, ranging from tiny pink petals to white blossomed shrubs to stately stalks of blue. I made a mental note to have Amos order a book on wildflowers for me. After twenty minutes, the trees opened up to a clearing, and I left the trail in search of an overlook. I dismounted and walked toward the edge of the meadow. Far below, a creek meandered at the bottom of a small canyon where I saw prospectors at three different sites. Trees in full, glorious foliage covered the hills up to timberline as deep crevices fell from the peaks in every direction. I drank in the view for a few moments and then remounted and climbed higher. I was in pure heaven, riding my horse in a panorama of beauty.

Life was going well. Ma brimmed with a renewed vigor. The pride of having her own business agreed with her, despite the hard work. As for myself, I felt ever on the edge of discovering new possibilities. Further along the trail, I peered down another canyon and saw two men digging at a surface showing. Jonas liked to talk about the recent discoveries even though, in truth, he had no inclination for mining himself. He said surface veins were rare and often turned out to be shallow deposits of minerals that were soon exhausted. The exception was the Mineral Farm Mine. One of the first mines in the area, it began shipping ore shortly after its discovery a year before. Unbelievably, the deposits of minerals there lay in exposed rows and were mined in ditches. The Mineral Farm was the rare exception: minerals were usually found in fissure veins that could run for miles, the veins ranging from an inch to the bonanza find of two feet wide. Miners exerted backbreaking energy to tunnel deep into the mountainsides. The thought of working long hours underground without the light of day gave me goosebumps.

The clouds gathered during the afternoon until the sky became a morose solid-gray blanket. The smell of rain signaled the end of the day's sightseeing as the wind spun up and heavy drops struck the dry earth. I was drenched by the time I arrived to stable my horse and vowed to never venture into the mountains again without a long slicker, which I planned to purchase with my next paycheck.

The following week, I experienced the excitement of a new mining town. A man greeted Mr. Dunnick just outside his office door. His name was William B. Freeland, and he was beside himself, spilling the news of his discovery just a few days before — June 28, to be exact. It was just below a high mountaintop at 12,300 feet, according to the aneroid barometer. He named it the "Virginius Mine." Silver was the predominate mineral, but it also contained gold.

Mr. Freeland placed his order for twenty burros to take supplies up to the new mine. The assayer's determination was so grand that Freeland was going to hire a dozen men to begin work there. He showed the assay paper to Mr. Dunnick to assure credit for the many burros he would be using for months to come. First, there would be weeks of hauling mining and food supplies up the mountain. Confident of its value, Freeland anticipated bringing the ore down the mountain. He would be doing business with Dunnick's for a long time to come.

I found the man's enthusiasm contagious, bubbling over onto me.

"Jonas, it's so exciting! This man will be rich soon."

"Well, there's plenty of time an' sweat 'fore that ore makes it down, but, yes, it looks like he'll be a wealthy man. I pity the miners workin' there in the winter, though, challengin' the elements that near the heavens."

The exuberance of this discovery stayed with me. I determined to do some prospecting myself.

The town had received tragic news of the battle at the Little Big Horn in the Dakota Territory. On June 25, two-hundred and sixty-two men died. People were in an uproar when they heard of it, talking about how all the red devils should be killed once and for all. It was a horrible event, but most seem to forget how the government had broken treaty after treaty with the Indian people.

Maggie's Way

When I think about how much I love the mountains, I believe I have an inkling of how these people must have felt when being driven from the land they had lived in for generations. As in the Rocky Mountains, thousands of miners had invaded the Black Hills in search of the shiny metal that caused so much upheaval. I grieved over all the dead victims of this battle, both white and brown.

Our local Ute Indians had been dispossessed here as well. In 1873, the Utes allowed the whites to take over the San Juan Mountains but kept the land to the north and west. On several occasions, I have seen small groups of Utes in town trading blankets or food. I have heard that the Utes are more peaceable than most Indian tribes, but perhaps they have simply become resigned to the inevitable conquest of their land.

My mother was not the only female entrepreneur in town. A handful of women started boarding houses, catering to the ever-growing influx of men who needed a place to sleep and a homemade meal. Many men took advantage of this luxury on trips back to town after weeks in the mountains, living in the crudest of styles.

I had the privilege of meeting one of these enterprising women quite unexpectedly. Jonas assigned me to deliver a freshly saddled mare down the road to a place identified by the sign, "Le Grand Monarque." When he insisted on the large black beauty that was one of our best mounts, I knew this had to be someone influential in town.

I tied the mare to the rail out front and entered the recently built log cabin. I came to the realization I was standing in a formal parlor room. Deep maroon velvet curtains, French provincial style upholstered sofas, and even a small organ transformed the crude log cabin. A young woman draped in a green satin gown with rows of lace and a revealing bodice reclined on the sofa. Upon seeing me, her lips slowly parted in a smile, and she winked at me. I understood at once in what kind of establishment I stood. I glanced down at my dusty trousers and heavy men's boots.

Hoping to avoid any misunderstandings, I declared my business.

"I — I'm here to deliver a horse!" I blurted.

She rose and meandered up to me anyway. She threw her hip to one side, one hand at her waist, caressing my shoulder with the other. The smell of thick, sweet perfume choked me. I gagged, coughing in her face.

"You are a young one, ain't ya," she said, her ebony-lined eyelids drawing low. Her English was broken with an accent I could not identify.

My legs shuddered, straining to run.

She smiled and winked again.

Another woman entered the room. Adorned in a more elaborate manner of dress than the former woman, she wore yards of crimson velvet, satin, and white lace. Rouge stains traced her high cheekbones and led to lips painted cherry-red. Her dark hair was done up in a fashionable arrangement of both upswept hair and loose tendrils falling onto her narrow shoulders. She was an attractive, mature woman and would have been prettier without the painted face. Her eyes narrowed at me as she stood with her hands on her hips, studying the dirt film that covered my face from sweeping out stables that morning. My stained clothes reeked of manure and horse sweat; it did not pay to wash them often as the dirt and smell of the stable returned in one day's work.

Her voice surprised me with its sultry, low octave tone.

"So Dunnick's has become so hard up they have to hire women now."

Her eyebrows arched high and reminded me of a bully ridiculing a smaller child. I decided right then I abhorred the woman. Meanwhile, the younger woman's face had swung up in shock.

Before I could speak, the older woman spoke again.

"Now why would you want to work in the dirt and manure when you could work in a pretty place like this?" Her arm stretched out in an arc, sweeping the room. One eyebrow remained cocked.

I was not sure if she was mocking me or recruiting me, but I notified her about the horse tied out front and turned on my heels to leave.

"Why are you leaving so soon, pretty boy?" the younger woman's voice rang out.

I glared at her. As I headed to the door, the women exploded in laughter. I slammed the door behind me and marched up the road to Dunnick's, my Irish blood boiling.

I arrived at the stable in record time and strode up to Jonas, not caring if my hot face was crimson.

"Why didn't you warn me? Jonas, I thought you were my friend."

Jonas's eyes averted mine like a child being scolded.

"Sorry, Miss. I didn't know how ta explain it, an' I surely didn't want ta enter that place myself."

I could tell he was remorseful. I imagine the fact that he was black would not have prevented those women from a business proposition.

"Don't surprise me like that again," I reprimanded.

And he never did.

18

MOUNTAIN HIGH EXCURSION

But Jonas did surprise me the next day with an unexpected offer. He got permission from Dunnick to take me on a packing trip destined for one of the remote mines. He knew how anxious I was to see a mining site. He had gone to a lot of trouble for me, and it was obvious he was trying to make up for his lack of judgment the day before.

He had one stipulation: since I had finally confessed to never using a gun, he insisted I learn to shoot. It was only a safeguard, he told me, but the hills were filled with wild and reckless men. And I was a woman, after all. I did not let on that I had already figured I should learn to fire a gun. I had seen many of these men around town. Some looked harmless enough, but I had seen others who leered at women on the streets, respectable ladies or not. Living as we were above Ma's restaurant on Main Street, many quiet nights were broken by the mayhem arising from the bawdy saloons. From the dens of gambling and booze, it was a brief walk to the houses of ill repute. Actually, many were just tents or shacks; not all were as fine as the cabin I had had the misfortune of seeing firsthand. Unfortunately, this new frontier included numerous saloons and brothels. Someone once told me that this was common in new mining towns. Along with the multitude of men seeking their fortunes came the saloon keepers and ladies of the night, eager to take the newly found fortune from them. Many were the men who squandered their valuable ore or sale of a small bonanza on women, cards, and drink. For those hungering for quick riches, they often made poor choices once they had hold of it.

Down by the river after work, Jonas showed me how to load the Colt .44 revolver, one chamber at a time. Then he taught me how to brace my arm to prevent the recoil of the pistol from putting me on my backside. I pulled the hammer of the single-action gun back with my thumb while I rotated the cylinder with the other hand. This set the trigger. Jonas said it was an accurate, well-balanced gun and operable even if parts of the mechanism broke. It seemed odd knowing parts of the gun could be so easily broken, but he said it was a common occurrence with the .44. Yet it was still the best revolver in the West. Jonas had purchased this partic- ular gun in 1873, the first year it was in production, and he was very proud of that fact. Holding my breath, I drew back the trigger. The recoil jarred me backwards, but I managed to keep from falling and making a complete fool of myself.

Walking back, we crossed the road just as a woman was leading a black mare up to the stable. It was the horse I had delivered the day before to the "ladies of the night." The young girl returning the horse was clad in a plain frock, buttoned high on the neck in a conservative manner.

"I'll take him off your hands, Miss," I said.

She was only a girl, thirteen at the most. The shy child said nothing and walked away.

Jonas insisted on target shooting every day after work. Surprising to both of us, I soon became very accurate. After a few days, Jonas gave me a few seconds before calling out a chosen target and expecting me to aim and shoot. Soon he was calling me a "crack shot."

In the early evening hours of that Fourth of July, I watched three leading businessmen speak a few words in front of a huge United States flag mounted on a hundred-foot pole on Main Street. It was the centennial of our country: one-hundred active, growing years. The brief ceremony having been conducted, it was on to the pressing business of a bustling mining town.

Walking home from work one evening, my mind was on Ma's good cooking, and I was considering a short ride after dinner when I passed Jud Abercomby. I greeted him and was met with a look of puzzlement. At last, his face showed recognition.

"Maggie?"

"How are you doing, Reverend Abercomby?"

"Why are you dressed like a young man?"

"I guess you haven't heard. I'm working at Dunnick's Freighting."

"That is far from a proper way for a young lady to dress . . ."

"It is not convenient to shovel manure in a dress, Reverend. Besides, I exercise the horses every day, and it would not be proper to have my ankles showing," I replied, trying to keep a rein on my emotions.

"I can see I am going to have to have a talk with your mother. If you want to be treated with respect, young lady, you will have to dress more ladylike."

"Good day, Mr. Abercomby." I hurried on before I lost my temper with a man of the cloth.

Later, while dishing up my dinner from the big cast-iron stew pot on the stove, I related the conversation to Ma.

Maggie's Way

"Reverend Harding did not seem to have a problem with your attire. It sounds like Reverend Abercomby needs to adjust to the frontier. If he wants a polished civilization, he's in the wrong place. Don't settle your mind on it, Maggie. He means well."

I did not say anything to Ma, but I decided then I would never attend any more of the man's services. That meant I was stuck with Harding's peculiar sermons. I put it behind me and savored my dinner, which included warm apple pie for dessert. This was a true delicacy as the imported canned apples came from Denver. I rattled on about the excursion Jonas and I would take to the mine the following day.

While preparing breakfast at dawn the next day, Ma and I caught up on each other's affairs. Our days were so demanding that, by the time evening came, conversation was limited. Ma painted descriptive pictures of the colorful characters that made up her clientele. One was the old man called San Juan Henry. He was one of the oldest prospectors around and was definitely a character. A soft rap at the back door sounded, and I went to the door.

"Good morning, Jonas. Come in. I'll bring you a fresh cup of coffee."

Jonas took his hat off and stood quietly. I handed him a steaming cup. He looked furtively in the direction of Ma flipping eggs and studied his cup before taking a sip.

"Where are my manners? Jonas, this is my mother, Margaret O'Malley."

Ma wiped her hands on her apron and extended her hand. "Glad to meet you, Mr. Johnson. Maggie has said many good things about you. I'm glad you could join us for breakfast."

"Glad to meet ya, Ma'am. Call me Jonas."

"Have a seat," I said. We usually ate at the small table in the back kitchen for our own meals. I set a bowl of hot biscuits and a large platter of fried potatoes on the table while Ma served up the eggs and bacon.

"Maggie has been so excited about this trip, Jonas. It's all she has talked about," Ma said.

"I 'av been up to see quite a few mines myself, but I know Maggie's achin' to see what all the fuss is about."

"I'll be eager to hear all about it when you return."

"Maggie was right. This is awful good food."

Ma laughed. "Thank you. I have been making it for years now."

"Does Maggie know how to cook?" he said, grinning.

"She certainly does. She just prefers to avoid it whenever possible," Ma answered.

"I prefer more exciting things, like looking for the silver and gold hidden in the mountains," I said.

Ma and Jonas shared a look. Jonas laughed, and Ma just shook her head. After filling up with Ma's substantial meal, Jonas and I walked in the dim early light down to Dunnick's. The stable hands were packing a mule by adding the load one side at a time, giving the animal a real struggle to keep its balance until the packing was completed. Some mules carried barrels of kerosene, others food, and a few packed crates of dynamite and blasting powder.

I proceeded to saddle my horse. Jonas must have readied his before breakfast, because he was already mounted outside. As the emerging light revealed a sky shrouded with clouds, I put on my new canvas duster and caught up with him. We rode at the front of the twelve-mule pack. Jonas called them a mule train because they traveled single file, harnessed together. The last mule had a bell tied to it to keep track of the end of the train on winding trails.

My freighting adventure was beginning. I was so excited, I feared I might burst. We were soon out of town and making the gradual climb from the bowl that formed Ouray. Although a man named Mears had been building a road in the San Juan Mountains, much of our journey would follow a narrow trail. We started up a draw, the town no longer in sight. As we rode side by side, Jonas enlightened me about the characteristics of mules. They made ideal animals for packing: their surefootedness combined with their strength made them fit for the narrow, steep trails in the mountains. They were also disease resistant, he added.

"I 'av heard of some mules livin' up to seventy years," Jonas said.

It seemed like a tall tale at the time, but I later learned it was possible. If cared for, they could live far longer than a horse.

Halfway up the mountain, the trees opened up to disclose a magnificent mountain looming above us. Wisps of clouds floated waif-like across the highest peaks. Although it was late July, snow remained in high crevices; Jonas said that, on some of the highest points, the snow never melts. Mountain peaks surrounded us in all directions, high gray-creviced rocks rising above timberline. To the west, thick trees capped a high ledge as cliffs descended in vertical grooves to the canyon floor. Farther on, below pine-covered slopes, canyon walls appeared painted in bands of ochre, sienna, and rust.

Rain drizzled throughout the day. At intervals it ceased, but drops continued to fall as they rolled off huge pine branches, making me grateful for my broad-brimmed hat. The moisture-laden air heightened

Maggie's Way

the smells of the forest: Crisp scents of moist earth and pine sap rose rich and full.

We did not see anyone, save for a lone prospector staying dry under a rock overhang. He studied our movement, knowing a mule train with supplies meant the discovery of a rich deposit. Whether it gave him hope or discouragement, I could not have said. Before we went out of sight, I looked back. His gaze remained fixed upon us.

The trail now led up a steep incline that turned into a very narrow rock ledge. Jonas urged me to ride ahead. On my right side was a high red rock wall, while just a few feet to my left was an enormous drop-off, plunging to a river below. Trying not to think what a spooked horse would do on such a precipice, I rode ahead. When I came to a wider section of the ledge, I turned my horse around to watch the progress of the mule train. Half of the mules were out of sight where the trail curved. The animals appeared unconcerned about either the height or the dangerous edge, just as Jonas seemed ever calm and confident. I continued up higher until I finally left the ledge. It was a relief to be on expansive ground once again. After Jonas caught up with me, I rode alongside him.

"They seemed to handle it calmly," I said.

"They 'av been on steeper. Snow is the real danger; if one animal lost its footin' and slid off, it could take the entire pack with it."

I didn't like to consider such an event. We continued to climb the mountain, the trail alternately curving, then straightening. There was ample time to evaluate the terrain, to see where the land dipped for a creek or rose to a stand of aspens, to examine the variety of wildflowers bursting up in the grasses, and to watch for birds and an occasional deer.

Eventually we climbed to just below the highest mountaintops. A rocky peak jutted out in stark contrast to the verdant hills around us; nothing grew on its slopes. Jonas called it "Stony Mountain." We now rode close to the creek that had shadowed the trail all along, though often from great depths below.

We came upon a man building a cabin and visited briefly with him. George Porter had plans of building a store, perhaps even creating a settlement here if mines kept appearing in the area. It was amazing to me that someone would consider a town at this height. From what Jonas had said, the snow could pile up fifteen to twenty feet in depth. The trail we had come up could never accommodate wagons, even during the summer months. I thought him mad, not unlike many struck by the mining fever.

We moved on and soon crossed the small stream. Jonas pointed out twin cascades in the near distance. The small Sneffels Creek here fed into the Canyon Creek we had followed during most of our journey. Flowers were abundant — violet columbines, red Indian paintbrush, and white clusters of yarrow. Ahead of us were the highest peaks in the area; Jonas claimed many were fourteen-thousand feet high. Crossing another stream, the trail veered, curving and dancing ever higher.

Suddenly we were in a bowl of flower-studded meadow grasses with dramatic rocky peaks towering over the amphitheater. Trees no longer grew at this altitude, where the heavens were close enough to reach out and touch. To the west, a rock peak dropped to a sheer cliff of pure ochre stone. The scenery was so dramatic, it was hard to believe we had been able to traverse this point of the mountain. Jonas said the mine was just around the bend, and a worn animal trail attested to this fact.

Rounding the hill, the Virginius Mine appeared on a steep mountainside blanketed with scree rock. The mouth of a shaft or tunnel — I could not determine which — was visible with thick logs framing the opening. Eight men milled around the hillside; several looked to be working on the early stages of an ore chute. Further on, the bottom layer of a log building had been started, possibly as a boarding house for the workers. A miner strolled toward us, his suit coat not unlike those worn by businessmen in town. I assumed he was the foreman. Upon closer inspection, his clothing was dusty, worn, and wrinkled.

He directed us past the mine opening and soon had the workers unloading the mules. I do not believe he looked at me long enough to avoid the mistake Jonas had on my first day of work. I unharnessed each animal after it was unloaded. Since it was late afternoon, we would not attempt the return trip today but start out the next morning. Soon, each animal grazed below in the luxurious grass of the amphitheater. The sight fixed in my mind's eye: magnificent peaks pressed against the heavens, jutting out all around me like assembled royalty. I felt at the top of the world here, as close to heaven as anyone could be.

Later, Jonas and I harnessed the mules and secured them for the night. We would take off at the crack of dawn. That evening, we ate with the foreman, Mr. John Haycock, who had invited us to a dinner of hearty venison stew at his campfire. He kept looking at me at intervals throughout the meal. I suppose he could not reach a conclusion about my gender, for he never said anything regarding the matter. Had not I, myself, seen young boys who appeared smooth-skinned and fair-featured?

He related that the ore extracted from the mine so far promised rich deposits of silver.

"You know," Mr. Haycock said, "all the seasoned prospectors and miners say: 'the higher you go, the richer the ore.' I believe there to be more to that than just old mountain lore. I'm convinced it's true."

I listened, spell-struck, to all his plans for the mine. They intended to work throughout the winter, which seemed unbelievable when I tried to imagine the amount of snow Jonas had described. Mr. Haycock had scheduled Dunnick's freighting straight through the summer and fall to stock up on all the supplies they would require. Once the snow came, the men would be bound here — not until spring would they be able to come back down to town. I wondered if they would survive. Maybe Ma was right: this mining fever was a disease that addled away at a man's brain. But it was fascinating, nevertheless.

That night, I surveyed the heavens from my bedroll under the stars. The three-quarters moon lit up the amphitheater, revealing the high rocky peaks lucidly above me. It was a wonder to see, but it was also unnerving. Perhaps it was the effect of the moonlight, but I felt we were trespassing. Looming over us, the grand heights defied submission to any mere mortal.

Mules loaded with winter stores. Sketches in the Colorado Mining Districts, North America. *The Illustrated London News*, Nov. 6, 1880

Maggie's Way

19

LADY PACKER

When Jonas came out of Dunnick's office, he was dabbing at the nervous sweat that threatened to run down his face. I feared it was bad news. Following our trip to the Virginius Mine, I implored Jonas every other day about my working with the pack trains. He soon realized I was not letting up any time soon about the matter. It became my burning desire, and I was going to do it, even if it meant going to every freighter in town and begging for a job. This morning he finally talked to Dunnick. I heard shouting coming from the office.

"He weren't none too thrilled with the idea, but said I could send ya on some small trips," Jonas said. "In two days ya'll 'av your stubborn Irish way. Don't make me regret it, gal."

I ran up and hugged him in delight.

"Now, it don't look good to be huggin' your boss, girl," he sputtered.

Later that night, I realized it may have been more than embarrassment that bothered Jonas. In the South, black men had been hung for the slightest contact with white women. Although this was the new frontier, men carried hatred and prejudices with them. I would never do that to Jonas again. The next day, I brought him a fresh apple pie in gratitude. I think he appreciated it far more than the hug.

That evening, I bubbled over as I told Ma my good news.

"Whatever were you thinking, girl?" Ma said. "What if something happened to you in the hills? I can see your shattered body lying at the bottom of a crevice." Ma's hands twisted the kitchen towel until it looked like a thick rope. It went through my mind that she might use it on me, grown though I was. She paced back and forth, from the stove to the table and back again, until she settled on the chair next to me. Ma's mouth set tightly as she gazed out the window.

"Ma, can't you see? I don't want to do anything else," I said. I stomped my boot against the kitchen chair. It skidded across the bare wood floor. "I can't work in a kitchen all my life; I'd die first."

Ma looked up sharply. For a moment, her eyes looked like a wounded puppy's after being beaten by its owner. I stared at the floor, my face hot as I regretted my indignant remark.

"And those prospectors," she continued, as if she hadn't heard. "I've seen those shifty characters . . . a lone woman deep in the mountains . . . oh, girl . . . and Amos won't be there to help you." Tears shone from my stalwart mother's eyes, marking only the second time I had ever witnessed her cry. I had never seen her worry like this before.

"Ma, I'll be careful. I promise." I said. "I'll have a gun."

"Oh, Maggie," she moaned, "if I lost you too . . ."

"You won't, Ma. You won't."

My first packing trip consisted of five donkeys loaded with food supplies and tools for a new mine close to town. It was an easy day trip, and Jonas could expect me back well within the daylight hours. He made me pack the animals by myself and did not give me any slack. I led the one haltered donkey as I rode my mare. The rest followed his lead through town. Once I found the trail leading to the mine, I untied the lead rope and allowed my small entourage to follow the trail. Packing donkeys was far different from mules, which were always tied together single file. This was like herding sheep. As long as I kept them going in the right direction, all was fine. I knew this was an easy job any respectable young lad could do, but I also knew it was meant to earn Jonas's trust in me. Besides, he had stuck his neck out for me with Dunnick. A woman mule skinner or burro puncher was almost unheard of in the West, although I had heard tell of a German woman down by Durango who ran mules.

I had tucked my braided hair up under my hat and rubbed dirt over my face before setting out. Although I knew I could not hide my gender from everyone, I was not going to give the appearance of "pretty" in any way. Jonas insisted I wear a revolver at my side.

I was proud to arrive at my destination with no mishaps, having adhered to Jonas's directions. I dismounted and walked up to the three men that comprised the entire working force of this new site. When I spoke, their eyes grew round as melons. Of course, my voice would always give me away.

"Well, I'll be darned, if it ain't a woman packer," the oldest one said.

Once they were over their surprise, they told me they were going to build a cabin during the next month so they could live next to their mine. It was not only for the sake of convenience; they also wanted to stand guard over their investment. Two of the men appeared to be father and son. The other man I didn't like much; his eyes moved across my body like a side-winding snake. He kept grinning at me in a foul way, so I nonchalantly drew my hand into my open coat, pulling it just far enough back to reveal the handle of my revolver. Pretending I didn't notice, I saw the

Maggie's Way

astonished look on his face, which soon turned to a noticeable scowl. Jonas was right: a gal had to be prepared in these hills.

After helping them unload the packs (but never turning my back to those strangers), I was soon herding the donkeys back down again. It was a glorious day, this first day as a freighter, and I was heady with satisfaction. Nearing an open meadow, I began to cross a stream. A man was excavating on a nearby hillside. He was alone, and I dared to call out to him, "Any luck today?"

The man stood up and turned to face me. Who in the tarnation should it be, but Matthew Harding! Recalling the moment later, I am sure my mouth was gaping open.

"Well, if it isn't young Maggie O'Malley with a turn in her career plans."

I frowned. Harding grinned, and his eyebrows arched as if I was a grand joke sent for his benefit. He was awfully cocky for a man of the cloth. Besides, a minister who looked for ore? Worldly riches? Perhaps he was a charlatan who liked to mine the offering plates as well.

"Do not look so shocked, Miss O'Malley. Just as you have a rather unconventional occupation, a shepherd can have side interests too," he said.

I had to give him that, though I still resented that mocking grin he seemed to wear at my expense.

"To answer your question, I have found an inconsequential streak of silver today. How has your journey been?"

My ckeeks grew warm, and I earnestly hoped my soiled face hid the coloring.

"Just fine, sir."

"You can call me Matthew."

My face grew hotter still. Then suddenly he was laughing. Had my blushing face betrayed itself after all?

"It appears as if your companions are more eager to return than yourself."

I looked ahead in dismay to see all five donkeys were far ahead on the trail. I set my horse into a run and left that detestable preacher far behind.

Maggie's Way

20

BUMBLING INSECT

Seeing Harding out prospecting gave me a nudge. It quickened the interest started when the old prospector, Johann, had shown me how to pan for gold. My next day off found me heading toward the mineral-rich slopes at dawn.

The early morning was a time of delight for me: everything was so fresh. Shadows flung themselves across the grasses, and flowers were wet with dew. Alert eyes could see deer and elk as they ventured into open meadows or drank at a brook. I found a quiet stream half a mile back into the forest from the lower valley of the sleepy town.

Tying my horse to a small aspen tree, I left a length of rope long enough for her to graze. I untied a pick from the back of the saddle and removed a steel pan from the saddlebag. Using the rocks rising above the ice-cold creek as stepping stones, I placed my thick boots on the larger rocks.

About a third of the way across, I sat nearly on my heels and scooped the gravel and small rocks from the creek bottom into my pan. With the water level up to the very rim, I sloshed it around, letting the heavier gravel settle to the bottom while the lighter gravel washed over the side of the pan and back into the creek. I continued doing this until most of the water was gone, then added more water from the stream and repeated the action. Each time the water dropped low in the pan, I studied the remaining fine gravel for metal. I worked the area for half an hour until I decided I needed to move further upstream, being sure to keep my horse in sight.

Judging by the angle of the sun, an hour had passed. I had not found any gold "flour," — as some called the tiny particles found in panning – least of all any gold nuggets. I walked back to my horse. I laughed and felt rather foolish, thinking I could find a golden treasure so quickly when men scoured the hills for months on end with no success. Many of them lived out in these hills because it took so long to look, dig, and search for their riches. If it wasn't hidden, all the ore would have been discovered by now, considering the number of prospectors in the hills. I untied my horse and moved further upstream to work another section. Since I had set out that day just to work the streams, I was willing to give it an honest effort.

My diligence went unrewarded. I worked for another hour, finding nothing. At last, I remembered the lunch packed in my saddlebag and stopped for a quick meal. Then it was back to panning.

When the sun was just below the peaks, I decided I had not seen Ma much, what with us both working so hard. I headed back, thinking that I would help out in the kitchen in hopes of persuading her to go for a walk with me that evening.

The church was holding a social for its faithful flock. They had gathered enough people who played instruments to put together an impromptu band. Ma had offered her restaurant, which made a large enough area once the tables were stacked against one wall, with the chairs lining the remaining walls. I didn't know how to dance, but I put on a dress and decided it would be fun to watch the others. Ma insisted on fixing my hair, drawing it high on my head with ribbons, tendrils falling over each cheek. I humored her as she created finger curls on each side.

By seven o'clock, people began to arrive. We set out plates of cookies and supplied hot coffee and honey-sweetened tea throughout the evening. The musicians warmed up their instruments while several women brought pies and cakes to add to the refreshment table. Reverend Harding arrived and greeted Ma while I tried to stay out of speaking distance by busying myself with arrangements in the kitchen. The man had a knack for making me feel uncomfortable.

People continued to pour in. The men had thought of everything; they took turns manning the front door in pairs. No one partaking in the spirits would be given access, solving the problem of drunkards wandering in from the nearby saloons. I saw Amos enter just then, looking a bit out of place. Ma had invited him, regardless of the fact he had not come to a service yet. I hurried over to greet him.

"Hello, Amos. How are you?" I said.

"Keepin' busy enough. It's good to see ya, Maggie." He looked at me and smiled. "I almost didn't recognize ya, but you sure look pretty."

"Ma insisted."

"I haven't danced since I was a young man," he murmured. His gaze took in the dance floor, and his eyes were glassy as if watching something from the past.

"I've never danced other than an Irish jig I learned as a child."

By eight, the house was packed full of men, women, and children. The musicians' instruments included two fiddles, a harmonica, and a guitar. Hand clapping and foot stomping added to the beat, making the floor vibrate wildly. I watched the married couples dance. They made it look easy, as if their feet floated over the wood floor.

Matthew Harding made the rounds of the room, greeting each of his parishioners. I noticed the young girls of fourteen and fifteen years old flitted about him throughout the night like bumblebees around a wildflower. I scrutinized him: I had to admit he was rather good looking once cleaned up, and I suppose the fact he was a man of the cloth made him a good marriage prospect. As if that was all there was to life — marriage and raising a bundle of babies.

Dancers packed the floor, with children on the outskirts swinging to their own beat. Amos asked if I wanted to learn the two-step. I hesitated, but the look on his face did not leave me the heart to disappoint him.

"It might take me a while to recall it myself," he warned.

I had told Ma earlier in the day that I had no intentions of dancing, but she insisted on telling me the secret was to stand on the balls of your feet, relax, and follow the man's lead. I took a deep breath and tried to do just that for Amos's sake. Poor Amos looked so nervous that I forgot to be embarrassed myself. Lost in the crowd, he relaxed at last and remembered the old steps of his youth. We were soon caught up in the joy of the music. After a couple of dances, Amos was off to find Ma to show off his renewed dancing ability. I walked over to the refreshment table and ladled out a cool drink of water from the bucket. A young girl about eight years old stared up at me.

"Hello," I said. "Are you having a good time?"

"Are you the woman who works with donkeys?"

"Yes."

"Why do you do that?" Her eyes stared, as if I was a strange circus act.

"I like working around animals. Besides, I enjoy getting out in the mountains. How about you?"

"But you're a woman . . ."

I chose that moment to go to the kitchen to see about brewing more coffee. It seemed even the faithful considered me an oddity. I filled the huge enamel kettle with fresh water, added more wood to the stove, and returned to the dance.

I found my foot tapping to the music and realized I longed to dance around the floor again. The young men were choosing to dance with girls of fourteen and fifteen years of age. I'm sure I was seen as an anomaly — being almost an old maid — for not having any suitors. The young men

Maggie's Way

didn't see me as a good marriage prospect, as I didn't fit the traditional role of a young woman. That was fine with me, since I wasn't looking for marriage. But how I wanted to dance just then.

Later, I did get my wish when asked to dance by some older men in their thirties. One was a widower, the other a bachelor who had never married. The latter had no sense of rhythm, and it was all I could do to muster enough Christian charity to finish the dance after he stepped on my feet several times. The widower kept telling me how pretty I looked, later adding how strong I must be to work as a freighter. I felt I was being sized up for the role of industrious wife and made a note to avoid him. A shy eleven-year-old boy approached me. "Would ya care to dance, Miss?" His eyes looked down at the wooden floor.

"Certainly," I said. "What's your name?"

"I'm Carl Bennett." He blushed slightly, studying his boots.

"Shall we?" I offered my hand.

He grinned up at me and put his arms in the proper positions. Someone had taught the young man how to dance. Carl was too young to care about my odd reputation. He was rather cute, blushing the entire time we danced. After the dance ended, he had me promise him another one later. I stood, watching the crowd on the dance floor for a while. When I looked around the room, everyone seemed to enjoy the evening whether they were dancing, eating, or visiting. I heard the musicians strike up another lively tune.

"Miss O'Malley, are you enjoying yourself this evening?"

I looked up to see the face of Matthew Harding. Darn, I had tried so hard to avoid him that evening…but I put on a smile and behaved myself.

"I have enjoyed the music," I answered.

"And some dancing, I've noticed." That same blasted grin.

"It's my first dance, and I'm afraid I'm not very good at it."

"From what I observed, you do quite well for a beginner."

The band started a new song, and he took my free hand, my other still holding a cup of water.

"May I have the pleasure of this dance?"

I began to protest but happened to notice a few of the young "bees" gathering behind Reverend Harding. I noted their faces registered disapproval as they saw him talking to me. I remembered the young girl's comment earlier and set my cup down.

"I would be delighted." I looked back at the younger girls and smiled. I admit I was being a bit devilish.

At least I had a chance to dance again before the night was over. I had decided that I was a wonderful dancer until I realized it was my partner. This man knew what he was doing; it was the smoothest dancing I had experienced all evening, and I liked it. Before I knew it, we had danced three songs in a row, and I no longer avoided his eyes. They were light blue, like a soft early morning sky.

"You look very nice tonight, Maggie," he said, as the music stopped.

I looked at him and thought for the second time that evening that the man was a bit handsome. My face became warm then, and I averted my eyes. A picture formed in my mind of myself in an apron with two babes clinging to my legs and one in my arms. I shook myself. I was determined to remind him of what an oddity I was to most people in town.

"I did some panning yesterday up in the hills, after a day off from mucking out the stables," I said. "How has your luck been lately?" I felt like myself again — the woman with trousers and heavy boots — despite the pink and blue flowered dress I presently wore.

"That's what I like about you, Maggie," he chuckled. "You are always a surprise to me. In fact, placer mining is fruitless unless you leave the mountains and head out for the valleys. Your chances will be better where the streams have washed the gold down."

I scowled, feeling humiliated. My distrust of the man was turning into dislike. He may have misread my emotion as disappointment, for he asked if I would care to accompany him the next day to a likely spot a few miles north of Ouray. In the midst of my confusion and embarrassment, I agreed, what with my mind being on prospecting as it was.

He paused for a moment as if considering something. "Perhaps your mother could come with us, and we could have a picnic. It is a beautiful spot."

Of course. How would it look to his parishioners to be out in the mountains alone with a young woman? It would have been jeopardous to his reputation as a man of the cloth.

"I will have to ask her..." I was already regretting my impetuous answer.

"I will pick you and your mother up at noon tomorrow then." He smiled and brushed my arm as he walked away.

I figured that, at the least, Ma would have a good time, and I could learn more about how to find gold. It was not until later in bed that I recalled dancing with him: how we glided across the floor, how his hand felt on mine, the strength of his shoulder beneath my left hand. I felt like one of those foolish bumblebees and lamented my agreement to his invitation . . . and he hadn't even waited for my mother's answer. How presumptuous the man was!

21

THE OUTING

Threatening clouds were my desire for the next morning, but, instead, I awoke to sunlight pouring through the small upper-floor window. I pulled the patchwork curtain aside. Sure enough, not a single cloud was visible.

Helping Ma in the kitchen didn't make the time go by any faster. In between orders, she prepared our picnic lunch of fried chicken, potato salad, and a special treat of blueberry pie.

"It's nearly eleven, Maggie, and you're not dressed yet."

"I am ready, Ma." I was wearing my trousers, a shirt, and my heavy boots. The only thing wanting was my big droopy hat.

"To a picnic, dear, with a young man?" Ma inspected my attire, a tiny frown growing between her brows.

"It's not that kind of picnic, Ma. We are both interested in prospecting, and he's going to show me a good site today," I answered.

"When a young man asks a girl's mother to go on a picnic, he has an interest in that young lady." Ma didn't wait for a rebuttal, but left to prepare another pot of coffee.

I went to fetch my horse, saddle up, and bring him back to the hitching post outside the restaurant. Ma, of all people, should have understood. She waited for a long time to marry. Where did it get her but soon widowed in a strange place with a baby to care for? No, marriage did not seem like a good bargain the way I looked at it.

I no sooner had my horse hitched to the post than I saw Harding coming down the street, bringing an extra horse for Ma. I took a deep breath. If he was expecting a pretty dress, he was in for a surprise.

"Good afternoon, Maggie," he said. "It is a fine day for an outing."

"Good day, Reverend Harding." I looked up briefly and then continued to adjust my horse's cinch.

"You must call me Matthew." he said, with a chuckle, "I see you are dressed for some arduous prospecting today."

My head jerked up.

"Were you expecting frills and lace?" I snapped, my hands braced at my hips.

"Maggie, I wouldn't try to predict you for one minute."

Good, I thought. Just as I would have it.

He reached into his pocket, then held out his hand.

"I brought a nugget for you to see."

I left my horse, walked over, and peered into his hand.

"You can hold it," he said.

I gingerly reached for the golden metal but jumped when he closed his hand over mine.

He laughed. "You have to say my name."

I rolled my green eyes at him, but soon my attention was back on the nugget.

"Matthew Harding, let go of my hand."

He let go with another laugh. It was the first nugget I had ever seen. Rounded from much rolling through the stream, it had several smooth lumps protruding from it. It was small, about the size of a pea.

"How much do you think it's worth?" I looked up to see him studying me.

"I am sure I could buy the town."

I shook my head at him. "I'll go tell Ma you're here."

Ma felt confident in leaving her help in charge for the afternoon. It was her first outing since we had arrived in Ouray, and she was thrilled to be seeing new sights. I soon forgot my regret about the occasion: it was worth every smile I saw on Ma's face that day.

We reached the site at last. Harding showed us the spot where he had found the nugget, and we began panning there. Ma watched me pan for gold, curious of the procedure. After I shook my third panning, I hollered in excitement. Harding was soon beside me. I held out the pan. Like a necklace, tiny bits of metal flakes strung themselves almost halfway around the bottom of the pan.

"That is something," Ma said with genuine appreciation.

I gave her the delicate task of retrieving the flakes and placing them in my little glass vial the old prospector had given me. Harding had brought an additional pan, so I used that in the meanwhile.

"This is great fun," I told him. We had a good site, after all — a second reason for being glad to have accepted his invitation.

"I am glad to have the privilege of being with you on a lucky day," he said. "It is worth my gold nugget to see you smile."

I gave up worrying whether he wanted something from me other than shared placer mining. I had a feeling I could learn a lot from him.

Maggie's Way

After a few hours, we stopped for lunch. Reverend Harding raved about Ma's cooking, which I could see pleased her. I was glad I had not prepared it, as that would have given the wrong message: the old adage of the way to a man's heart and all.

"Matthew, where does your family live?" Ma asked.

I knew this was for my benefit, an attempt to get to know Reverend Harding better. He revealed that he had been on his own since the young age of eleven after running away from a deplorable orphanage. Any shirt-tail relatives had been too far away. For all practical purposes, they did not exist. Then my curiosity got the better of me, and I asked a question that had long intrigued me.

"How did you become a preacher?" I watched him with an eye of scrutiny.

"When my ma was alive, she used to say I sure talked a lot for a little boy, so I suppose preaching comes natural for me." He winked. "Truthfully, a traveling preacher took me in when I was on my own. Unlike some who preach to rake in the money, William was honest and sincere. I stayed with him until he died of consumption. I loved that man like my own father, and I would still be with him if he had lived."

There was an uncomfortable pause. I sneaked a peak at Ma and saw moisture shining in the corners of her eyes. I looked at my feet then, not wanting to embarrass him.

"He was the kindest man I ever knew," he continued. "He taught me a lot about living, and about dying too, I guess. But that's enough about me. How about another piece of that wonderful pie, Mrs. O'Malley, and then Maggie can tell me how a nice young woman becomes a grizzly old packer in the great San Juan Mountains."

I probably deserved the remark.

Matthew taught me that day how to watch for the colors of rocks. Greens and blues indicated copper, transparent quartz was often associated with gold formations, while red, rusty rocks showed signs of iron. We continued to pan for another hour and a half, but to no avail.

"There is always another day," I said. My humor had improved since that morning. Perhaps I had judged him unfairly; he was not such a bad character after all. Maybe by now he realized I was not marriage material. Then again, perhaps he was content to remain an unmarried man.

"Does that mean, Maggie O'Malley, we can go prospecting again?"

That same twinkle in his eye and cocky smile did not annoy me for once. I had found a prospecting partner. Who would have guessed from a preacher man?

22

PACKERS, MINERS, AND SOURDOUGHS

It is hard to change a man's mind, and Dunnick still thought freighters should be men. I may have spent most of my time mucking stalls and pitching hay had it not been for one of the freighters becoming ill. When times get tough, exceptions are made, and it helped get my foot in the stirrup, so to speak. Again, I was assigned only the burro expeditions. I was not insulted, but decided I would let time prove my ability. So far, I had run up as many as twenty loose burros and carried loads of equipment, food supplies, and long pieces of lumber with one end trailing in the dirt. Jonas told me miners ordered the lumber a bit longer in anticipation of losing part of what dragged over the ground.

I grew to appreciate the burros. They had their own mind at times, granted, but they were also steadfast workers. I knew many freighters abused their animals, but I practiced patience, not wanting to be cruel to any animal. After a while, I learned to trust them when they hesitated or balked, finding they usually had a good reason for their action. One day, I had come up from behind to see why they had stopped, only to find the trail washed out from the previous day's rain. I found a detour around the spot, and we were soon on our way again. If a person respected an animal's spirit, it performed better in the end.

Between my packing trips into the mountains and prospecting on my own time, my sourdough friends were growing. I trusted my instincts on whether a prospector proved a threat to me. After a few minutes of conversation, I had a good idea whether he was someone I should avoid or a person I would talk to next time around.

One day while I was packing my Rocky Mountain Canaries, as the burros were called, I came across an old prospector coming down the trail I was aiming to go up. As we neared each other, I stopped and visited with him a bit. He was not a person one would soon forget. His thick, gray hair took on a bush-like effect against his long, narrow face. His chin jutted out to such an extreme point that his mouth appeared to sink back in direct opposition to the force of the chin. When he spoke, it about startled a person, so high-pitched it was, with a funny twang of an accent I could not place. When he smiled, a gaping mouth revealed three lone teeth. I soon discovered his name was Henry; he was quite a chatty old pickle. He asked all about me and how I had gotten into freighting.

"These hills are alive, you know," he told me, "brimming over with riches that could let a man spend the rest of his days in luxury."

It was easy to know who had gold or silver fever and to what extent. Henry was a dyed-in-the-wool believer in sudden fortune and claimed he was a lifelong prospector. He had been in these hills since 1861, and, before that, he had lived on the Front Range. He pointed out that many of the paths throughout the San Juans had begun as Indian trails, while the crudely built bridges used to traverse the creeks were evidence of the more recent prospectors.

Back in town, I learned that Henry was well known by anyone who spent time in the hills. Better known as San Juan Henry, as Ma had identified him, he was famous for his storytelling and his knowledge of local history. People said some of these old codgers hid away their riches and continued to live a solitary life in the wilderness, which was closer to their true love than wealth. After talking to Henry, I believed it possible.

On one freighting trip, I came across a prospector whose wife accompanied him. They were a middle-aged couple whose children evidently had left home, leaving them the freedom to hunt for their fortune. I saw them a ways off the trail and, by their wary looks, they did not appear to welcome company. Later I was to learn about claim jumpers and how that might make people leery of strangers.

The month of July passed, and August was soon upon us. August 1, 1876, was a big day for Colorado, as it became the thirty-eighth state. We all talked about it, but the town was too busy to celebrate the fact.

Two weeks later, I went prospecting with Matthew Harding once again. This time he did not ask Ma along, not that it mattered to me. I was not one for formalities, but I was curious, as he was a preacher and all. So, I inquired.

He laughed.

"I do not expect, dressed as you are, most people would think I was in danger of improprieties."

I knew people saw me differently, especially women, and he was probably right about the way people looked at things. I had a hunch that as a preacher he tried to respect traditions, but deep down, he was not all that concerned about the outward appearance of things. As we rode side by side, I took notice of the fact that he looked like a bona fide prospector. A pick and shovel were tied to the back of his saddle, and a pan stuck out of one of the saddlebags as he rode his bay quarter horse down the dirt road.

Half of the pleasure of mining was the ride to and from the site: the fresh smell of pine, my body moving to the even rhythm of the horse, the sound of small creeks bubbling over river rocks, the sunlight and shadow playing hide and seek under the forest canopy. All these things were pure enjoyment in themselves. Today we rode to a different site, new horizons ever the aim of the prospector.

We decided on a hill overlooking a stand of aspens. Their white bark reflected the light, and broken branches and natural scars left interesting black "eyes." At times, I caught the scent of the wood, a unique, sweet smell.

We worked on a rock overhang. The day was warm as August can be, and Harding removed his heavy outer shirt, revealing a faded, long-sleeved red undershirt beneath the suspenders. For a man who did not do heavy physical work, he retained a strong look in the shoulders and arms. He caught me watching him. I turned back to my pick. I looked sideways and saw one of those characteristic grins as he continued to heave his pick into the rock layers.

We broke for lunch. He surprised me the day before by offering to bring the food. I have to admit, whether it would be tasty or not, I liked the idea that he did not assume I would bring the meal. I brought a pie, though, as a small contribution in case the lunch was lacking. I watched as he unpacked the food, being inquisitive of the contents. He spread out a small gingham cloth on the grass and set up our lunch: buttermilk biscuits, dried jerky, fresh berries, and cheese.

"Did you make the jerky?"

"I did, and the biscuits too." He smiled as if he thought he had played a great joke on me by cooking.

"Let me see if it's any good," I quipped.

Jerky is jerky, I thought, but I could decipher some tasty spices. Surprisingly, the biscuits were not heavy as I expected. They were quite flaky.

"What is the verdict, my adventurous freighter?"

I gave my best pondering look.

"Well . . ."

"Oh, come now, it's not that bad."

I tried to mimic the notorious grin he always gave me at times like these.

"All right then, I will admit you can cook a bit."

"That's all the better you can do?"

I detected a note of disappointment in his voice.

Maggie's Way

"All right, it *is* good," I said. I reached out and patted his hand. His other hand reached to cover mine.

"I am glad you could admit it." There was that grin again.

My face grew warm from ear to ear. Without giving it much thought, I had enacted an indiscretion. His hand remained over mine. Looking down at the gingham cloth, I was angry with myself for encouraging the very thing I wanted to prevent. *Oh, how stupid you are Maggie O'Malley. Look at what you've done.*

Gold and Silver Mining, Colorado — A Honey-combed Mountain.
Drawn by Frenzeny and Tavernier. *Harper's Weekly* July 18, 1874

Maggie's Way

23

SILVER IS A GIRL'S BEST FRIEND

He withdrew his hand, as if he had read my thoughts.

"Your mother's pie is wonderful as usual. Please give her my thanks," he said.

"Ma was busy restocking food supplies, so I made it." I was pleased he thought it as good as hers.

"Why Maggie O'Malley, you're a woman of never-ending surprises." He picked up his hat. "Back to mining, gal," he said then.

I felt relieved.

Harding retrieved the shovel and showed me something new. He dug through to the bedrock and emptied the contents of dirt and stone to the side. Then he broke the rock into smaller pieces with the pick. He smiled, shrugged his shoulders, and asked me to try my hand at it.

Following his example, I took the pick. I was delighted to learn everything I could about prospecting. I repeated the process while he went upstream to get a drink, his hand cupped to his mouth.

"Look at this!" I yelled. "Come here!"

He hurried back to me, one eyebrow cocked.

"Look!" I held out a rock segment with silvery veins. My eyes locked on his, waiting for the reassurance that it was what I hoped. He picked me up off my feet and spun me around, then put me down at last.

"So, is it the real thing?" I asked.

"It is, and a fine thing at that."

"Yahoo!" I yelled loud enough to scare any wildlife in a mile radius. In my exuberance, I did a little Irish jig, then grabbed him and gave him a big bear hug. The next thing I knew, he bent down and placed his lips over mine. It was my first kiss. So this is what it felt like: warm, soft, so close I caught the scent of his skin.

He broke away, apologizing profusely. Strangely, I found myself irritated when he pulled back. Of course, I kept my ambivalent feelings to myself. He began digging more exploratory holes. I stood there, watching him for a moment, quite at a loss. Then I began working, soon able to forget my feelings and return to the excitement of finding silver again.

We continued working until the shadows grew long, and we realized we would have to return another day. We had collected a fair amount of silver in a leather bag Harding closed with a broken piece of rein leather. On the way back, he talked about us taking it to the assayer together the next day. We babbled on in our excitement. I had recovered my feelings from the unexpected kiss and brushed it off to the excitement of the moment. He had apologized, after all. My mind returned to the realization that I was truly a miner now.

The next morning I paced back and forth along the boardwalk, unable to contain my energy. I waited for Matthew Harding outside Ma's restaurant, anticipating the visit to the Assay Office. Had I slept last night? Fitfully, at best.

He came strolling up the street at last. I pretended not to see him until he came within talking distance.

"What took you so long, man?"

He looked at me with one eyebrow raised, grinning at me as usual. "Are you always this impatient?" He leaned against the hitching post as if he had all the time in the world.

I grabbed his shirtsleeve and urged him to hurry. I wanted to be first in line waiting for the office to open its doors. He laughed as if enjoying my anxiety.

We walked down to the Assay Office, which was located at the far end of Main Street, at the opposite end from Dunnick's. To my chagrin, despite the early hour, four people had preceded us. I looked up at Harding, who reassured me we had still beaten the throngs of miners yet to come. He pulled something out of his pocket: a piece of hard candy. As he held it out, the light filtered through the transparent colors and formed a rainbow effect. Candy was a rare thing for me, so it succeeded in diverting my attention.

One man waited with a small bag in hand, looking more like a farmer than a prospector in his overalls and straw hat. An older man with a long, untrimmed beard more aptly fit my concept of a sourdough. His soiled clothes had probably never been cleaned and would be replaced only when the seams no longer held. I assumed it was his mule tied up a short distance away. Another man ahead of us in line constantly shuffled his feet. He wore a long, canvas coat and a new beaver-skin hat. Perhaps the hat had been purchased with recent findings of ore, I thought as I sucked on the sweet candy. His eyes looked hard for one so young, and I was glad Harding was standing nearby.

Maggie's Way

It was the woman, though, that captivated my attention. The middle-aged lady dressed in a simple cotton print dress, with her hair piled severely on top of her head, waited solemnly. She looked familiar, but I could not place her. Obviously, it was not from services, or Harding would have greeted her.

Everyone waited silently, being around strangers as we all were, but it might have been due to the desire of each person to avoid speaking about their findings for fear of revealing too much about the site.

The door at last opened. The assayer must have come in through a back way, since the building was far too small to afford living quarters. The farmer fellow entered first, followed by the prospector. The woman remained outside next to the door, while the shuffler in the long coat paced back and forth under the fifteen-foot awning over the storefront.

Harding pulled out more candy, a piece for both of us, and we talked about the weather. He was becoming more anxious the closer we came to the reckoning. A small crowd was building behind us as the morning light became stronger. Ouray remained long in shadow as it waited for the sun to clear the high peaks each day. The straw-hat man came out looking dejected but trying hard to hide it. Later, the old prospector appeared, talking under his breath about more from where that came from. The woman then entered the building, the man with the long coat following her. Our feet landed on the porch at last, and Harding cracked the door ajar.

"There's room to wait. Let's go inside." He was now as nervous as I was.

Harding pointed out a small brick furnace in the back used for smelting purposes, which produced molten silver or gold. A long counter held crucibles and cupels, containers used in the furnace, and a variety of apothecary-style jars filled with fluxes used to mix the pulverized rock to aid in melting ore. On the wall hung tongs, sieves, a sledgehammer, and needle-nosed forceps. A bucking board held a muller used to crush the ore. Two men worked behind the counter. The taller man with a handlebar mustache stood at the assayer's scale, precisely weighing a small ore sample with brass counterweights. I never realized there was so much involved in determining the content of gold and silver in ore samples.

The woman waited, a black tapestry satchel resting on the counter.

"So you've been cleaning house again, I see?" the heavier man chuckled.

"A woman's work is never done, you know," she said. Her mouth parted with a brief smile, revealing one front tooth missing.

He handed the bag she gave him to the other man, who in turn poured the contents onto the scale. Fine particles of gold dust built into a peak. When he was finished, he murmured to the first man, who handed her the appropriate currency. She turned to leave, never glancing at anyone in the room, walking out with a self-satisfied look on her face.

At last the long coat quit pacing, as it was his turn at the counter, where he placed a large chunk of ore. The assayer said something, and the man cursed and stormed out of the office.

We walked over then.

"Green horn," he said as if in explanation.

"That woman looked so familiar, but I cannot place her..." I said.

Harding looked at me, astonished that I wanted to make small talk with the clerks at a time like this.

"Oh, that's Mrs. Hennigan who runs the boarding house down the street. She comes in once a week after cleaning up after her patrons."

"That's a good one, Harvey," the other fellow interjected.

The assayer realized by my blank face that I needed more in the way of explanation.

"When she sweeps the floor, the gold dust that has filtered from her boarders' bags, clothing, and boots is swept up. By the end of the week, she's sifted enough gold from the dirt to make herself a little extra income."

"That is something," Harding said obligingly, then slammed our bag on the counter. He glared at me, in warning of any more chitchat. After a prolonged wait, the assayer told us it was a good sample, and, if we could locate the source of the ore, we could be a very rich couple. I inwardly cringed at his assumption that we were married, but this was good news. We walked out, happy as larks. We remained silent until we were well away from the Assay Office.

"Did you hear that?" he said at last. He twirled me around just as he had at the creek. "We could be a rich pair!"

We were both as excited as children on Christmas morning. I laughed with all the enthusiasm of the moment, while hoping Harding was only referring to our mining partnership. We spent the next two months, on and off, tracing the source of the rich ore. Unfortunately, we never found it, but we didn't stay discouraged for long. Prospecting was in our blood now, and we were infected with the "fever."

Maggie's Way

Workmen in an assay office molding the melted bullion into bars.
Frank Leslie's Illustrated Newspaper, April 20, 1878

24

MULE TRAIN

It began with Abel running off to try his hand at prospecting. Then John had a mule kick him, and the final straw was when Arthur did not report to work for the fifth time that month. He was roostered again from his late nights at the saloon. All these mishaps proved the hand of Providence for me. Out of sheer necessity and frustration, Dunnick agreed to let me pack a mule train. I was to take Arthur's mules as scheduled; Dunnick walked away muttering something about how I could not be any worse than those no-good, unreliable men.

I was excited and apprehensive at the same time. It wasn't difficult to herd a bunch of loose burros, but would I be able to run a mule train? Dealing with fourteen mules harnessed together on the high, narrow trails to the remote Micky Breene Mine would be a new experience. Sweat began to bead up on my forehead as Jonas produced a map. He solemnly reviewed the twists and turns of the trail. Meanwhile, stable hands loaded the animals. There was no way I was going to betray my anxiety, but this was a true test. Would everyone have a good laugh at my expense? Then I might as well work for Ma in the restaurant or, worse yet, marry and be tied to my own apron strings the rest of my life.

The journey was set to proceed immediately. I sent word to Ma by having one of the men inform her of the trip and my scheduled return the next evening.

"Now you're goin' to find out if ya really wanna be a mule skinner," Jonas said to me, out of hearing of the others. "Be careful, gal."

Dunnick came out at last. He stood with both hands on his hips and watched my departure, likely regretting his decision already. My boot heels nudged my mare to walk out, the mules in a long formation behind me. Clouds of dust arose from the street, kicked up from so many hooves moving over the dry ground. The journey commenced whether I felt ready or not.

Once out of sight from Dunnick's, I studied the hand-drawn map to familiarize myself with the route. Whenever I came upon a junction or question of direction, I stopped to reexamine the map. Now that would be something, I thought, if I became lost or, worse yet, went to the wrong mine. I would become the laughing stock of the town, not to mention out of a job. With the fortitude of my Irish mother, I set out to prove myself.

Thankfully, the sky was a cloudless bright cobalt blue, giving me a measure of good attitude for the trip. I prayed often that first day. I etched into my brain the instructions that Jonas reviewed for controlling the mule train: use the jerk line attached to the lead animal by pulling once for a move to the left and twice for directing the train to the right.

I turned in my saddle and looked at the long line of tall ears behind me. A bell tied to the mule at the rear rang softly. I would later appreciate the ringing bell on winding trails, where the rear of the train was out of sight. Mules could take heavier loads than the smaller burro. Some animals appeared to be carrying the maximum weight, loaded with big wooden crates and kegs. Others were loaded with barrels of kerosene; some I was told, were loaded with dynamite.

After traveling a while, the train headed up the steep trail to the Micky Breene. There was no way to turn them around on the narrow path. The only option was to move upward along the steep precipice. If one mule slipped off the cliff, it would take the entire train. On top of this worry, dynamite could explode if a few animals pulled any shenanigans.

Near the highest point above the precipice, the lead mule refused to go further. My heart pounded double time. Most mule skinners at this point would show brutality, forcing their dominance. The mule skinners that worked for Dunnick were known for their crude language, due to years of battling the contrary animals. John's broken limb, for example, was not a simple accident. It was more likely retaliation for a cruel hand long remembered.

My tongue grew dry, and I broke out in a sweat. I dismounted from my horse. I stood there for a few minutes, looking at the stubborn mule. He stared into space, focused on nothing, and acted as if he didn't see me.

I patted the rump of my horse, sending her further up the trail. I took a deep breath and began murmuring to the mule, stroking his face and neck. Then I turned around and prayed he would follow my lead on foot. God's mercies, he did, and I walked the pack up the narrow trail about an eighth of a mile past the precipice. After that incident, the rest of the journey was inconsequential.

At last, I arrived. Mounds of expunged dirt and rock were visible a short distance from the mouth of the mine. The foreman raised a hand in greeting and walked over. Short in stature, he was solid and thick in the chest. When he was close enough to get a good look, his dark eyes narrowed. At last, he chuckled.

"O'Malley," I announced. "Are you the foreman?"

"Sure am," the man said. "Dunnick must be addled in the head if he's hiring women now."

"Your freight's here undamaged and on time," I said. "What do you have a problem with?" I looked hard into his eyes.

"Didn't mean no harm, just not used to seein' women freighters."

The man, named Butch, shouted for three workers to help unload the packs. A young man without any chin hair yet was working closest to me. He looked at me and smiled. "Some guys can't believe a woman can do anythin' but raise babes. I know different. My ma could break a bronc quicker than the best farm hand we ever had."

I could tell he was younger than me, and the freckles only added to his youthful appearance. He seemed like a decent guy.

"I'm Maggie." I extended my hand.

He shook it heartily and told me his name was Peter. "After a few runs, they'll get used to ya."

The ride back would be an easier prospect. The mine didn't have enough ore to transport yet, so both the mules and I relaxed on the way down. Heading down the trail, I had not traveled far when the foreman emerged on the downside of the trail, blocking the way. He was on foot and swaggered up close to me with shotgun in hand.

"My, my, the girlie packer and her mules . . ."

25

TROUBLE DOUBLED

With great effort, I drew my eyes up to the face of the man who held a gun on me. What I found there terrified me more than the dark, formidable eyes of the Remington's double barrels. The man's black eyes bored into mine. The foreman bellowed at me to get down off my horse, thrusting the barrels in my face. Not having a choice, I dismounted.

Just then, his squirrelly mutt of a dog jumped up on him. I called the detestable fool's bluff: I drew my pistol from beneath my unbuttoned oil-skin coat and cocked my revolver. His eyes lit up as he discovered it was aimed straight at his middle.

"Now, mister," I said. "You might kill me, but you're going down too. So, I'd slowly back away now and let me by."

For a moment he glared, sizing up the situation, but keeping his barrels on me. At last, he lowered the gun and held up one hand.

"Okay, Miss. I guess ya Irish are just stubborn enough ta die. Don't do nothin' rash, now . . . I'm leavin' . . ."

I never took my eyes or aim off him for an instant. Leading the mules down the trail, I never turned my back on the man, at one point nearly walking backwards. When at last he was out of sight, I remounted. I tried to quiet my racing heart and steady my shaking hands.

I continued on, never quite letting down my guard, ever feeling in danger of that hateful man. I'd set up camp sometime around dark, putting as much distance betwen me and the Mickey Breene as possible. I was determined to put an end to this day.

Autumn soon descended upon the high country. The aspens were beautiful after they had changed into their fall apparel. The bright leaves fluttered in the slightest breeze, explaining why they are often called "quakies." The gold foliage was a perfect foil against the alpine fir and white spruce on the hillsides. Earlier in the morning, I had attended church service. It was a day meant for getting out in the mountains to prospect and picnic, but I had soon learned that Matthew was obligated

94 &

Maggie's Way

to his parishioners after the services. Someone always invited him to a meal afterward, so I escaped the confines of town by myself.

After riding a ways, I decided it was the sort of day best enjoyed by not having any particular plans. I picketed my horse to a tree and walked through the woods. I came to a small creek and crossed over a shaky makeshift bridge, the type that was commonly seen in the hills.

Is there anything as glorious as walking over autumn leaves? Each footstep I took crushed the golden quaky coins, releasing the peculiar aroma of dry decomposing leaves. The hillsides were filled with miners churning the very bowels of the mountains in hope of a bonanza. To my way of thinking, the shimmer of golden aspens was the true Rocky Mountain gold. I found a lovely spot on a slope to view the valley below. Leaning against a white barked aspen, I closed my eyes and took in the fragrances drifting up from the forest floor.

"Hello, girl."

The loud, gruff voice was startling. My instinct urged me to spin around, but another part of me said move slowly and confidently.

I turned my head in the direction of the voice. There, not fifteen feet from me was Jud Abercomby. I had seldom seen him since I began working at Dunnick's. In the meantime, he had found another place to hold his services. His ruddy face stared at me in a manner too studied for my comfort. His large frame was clad in dark gray trousers and a matching vest under an open coat falling above the knees. His clothing was wrinkled and dusty. The short, turned up brim of his hat emphasized his glaring eyes. It was almost as if he had no recognition of me.

"Hello, Mr. Abercomby. Beautiful day, isn't it?" I forced myself to speak pleasantly. He stepped closer.

"Oh, that it is, my girl," he said, with a twisted grin.

I felt like a deer cornered by a cougar.

"I see you're back in your skinner clothes. I saw ya all gussied up for Sunday service. Ya might fool some people, but any gal who dresses like you do ain't no lady."

My heart was pumping out of control. I held my breath.

"But then, that's okay, gal. I know what ya really like."

His wide-open dark eyes looked me over while he sneered with a crooked smile. He stepped nearer.

That was too close for my comfort. My right hand swept to the revolver at my side. Before he knew what I was doing, I whipped out my Colt and brandished it in his face. I cocked the gun. It sounded like a felled tree tumbling in the deadly quiet forest. "Not one step closer, Mr.

Abercomby, or by my Lord Jesus Christ, I swear I'll fire." My body tensed, anticipating any sudden moves to overpower me.

"Now, I don't mean any harm, gal. Don't ya get trigger jumpy now, I'm goin'."

While moving sideways like a lobster, his beady eyes darted back and forth between the path of his retreat and my Colt aimed dead-on.

"Ya know I didn't mean any harm, me bein' a man of the cloth and all. Ya just put that pistol down now, I'm goin'."

There was no way I would lower my gun while he was within eyesight. In fact, I kept the firearm out in front of me for five minutes following his departure. It felt like déjà vu, so soon after the incident at the Micky Breene. I kept the gun handy after I began retracing my steps back to my horse. In the aspen grove where I was certain I had left her, Sierra had disappeared. In all the excitement, had I taken a wrong turn or forgotten where I had tied her? I looked around trying to figure which way to go, my trembling revolver still out in front of me. Could Abercomby be watching me? It was a possibility.

I studied the area; it seemed to be the right place. Then I saw the large quartz boulder I recalled seeing after I walked away from my tethered horse. A wild sunflower grew behind it so close its lower leaves brushed the rock. This was definitely the place. I walked back looking for the small tree to which I had tied my horse. I found it, sighting evidence on the bark of a slight abrasion worn by the leather reins.

I whistled loud and clear. Encountering only silence, I tried again. The quiet was shattered then by the sound of hooves pounding earth. Sierra trotted up to me. I placed my revolver back into the leather holster and reached into the deep pockets of my coat for a sugar cube. Henry Randall had taught me how to get my horse to answer to a whistle. Associating a treat with the whistle was a good way to train a horse to come rather than playing games trying to catch the animal. I would send a letter to Henry in gratitude for the tip.

Abercomby. He must have recognized Sierra; paints were not common, and mine was quite a beauty at that. Knowing I was not far away, he had his intentions planned. Abercomby figured I was alone and defenseless. I shuddered.

I rode back at a brisk trot, my eyes ever alert as I went. The beauty of the day was obliterated despite the bright sunshine, for the darkness in a human soul was terrifying. What made it far worse was the fact that this wolf was a shepherd in disguise, his true nature hidden to the townspeople. What other unsuspecting woman or young girl might be his next victim? How could I warn people in the community or, at least, in his own parish? What would I say? He had not touched me or said as much, but I knew instinctively he meant to do me wrong. There was no mistaking that. Unfortunately, there was no proving it either. Then, too, some might think I had encouraged it. There would be those who would not believe an unconventional young woman like me.

There was nothing I could do. It was a grievous realization that kept me from sleeping well for days.

🦅 26 🦅

THE HORSETHIEF

Packing burros to the Mineral Farm Mine, I was anxious to see this one-of-a-kind operation. Only five burros were required for the new mining tools John Eckles had ordered. This rich mine was located just outside of town, an uncommon occurrence at lower altitudes, but the real novelty was how this ore was deposited.

Upon arrival, the packs were unloaded, and I asked if I might see how the ore was procured. Men in town joked about the farmers that worked here. It was not long before I saw what all the joking was about. This ore ran at the surface level in parallel veins, eliminating the need for long tunnels and deep shafts. In truth, the miners dug the ore out of trenches. If I had not seen it for myself, I would have passed the talk off as grand exaggeration.

I watched as the miners stood in the full light of day, digging with picks and then shoveling the ore. Although Eckles and his partner, Begole, were the subject of much jesting, I realized it was in envy, for there never was another successful mine in the area like it. The expense of transporting ore over miles of narrow, high paths vanished. I was pleased to witness this unique mine.

The muffled thud of horses' hooves on soft earth broke the early morning stillness. Occasionally, a shoe rang out as it hit a rock embedded in the trail. The low light in the sky acknowledged our jump-start on the day. I watched Harding's back as he moved in rhythm with his horse. These outings together left me with an easy, comfortable feeling about the man.

Horsethief Trail was our destination, and this time prospecting was not on our minds. Well, perhaps we would keep our eyes half open, for it had become an ingrained habit to watch for the lay of the land and the colors in the streams. I had heard of the famous trail, and, between the two of us, we obtained adequate directions.

I ran into San Juan Henry a few more times during my packing trips. He told me this route was so frequented by the Spanish on their way through the Rockies that it was not uncommon to hear of travelers finding Spanish armor on the trail. He claimed its history dated back to the ancient Indians. Henry knew an old fur trader who had shown him very old arrowheads that, many years later, archaeologists called Clovis points. Our destination was the section of the trail that reached the top of the amphitheater overlooking Ouray.

Harding reined in his horse and turned back to look at me with that characteristic smile of his.

"Why is it called the Horsethief?" he asked.

I lit up with the satisfaction of knowing the answer, thanks again to old San Juan Henry. I pulled my horse up alongside his.

"Well, because of the horse thieves, of course," I said. "They stole horses from the San Luis Valley and used this trail to sell them in Utah."

"My little historian, tell me, were they Injuns?" His right eyebrow rose higher. The smile remained.

"Both white and brown thieves, according to my best source."

"And who might that be?"

"You know us packers, we do not reveal our sources." I gave him my best nonchalant smile.

He reached over and pulled my braid, drawing my head toward him. "Ouch!"

He kissed me before I could protest and then spurred his horse into a run. My hat had fallen off, so by the time I remounted, it took me a while to catch up. He began talking a mile a minute about someone showing a large nugget around town. He said each time the story was told the nugget enlarged by at least double the size. It was more than likely a myth of the bottle. I presumed he was teasing, about the kiss that is, for I did not want to take the time to worry about the implications.

By late morning, we were balancing on the Bridge of Heaven. We rode upon the narrow bridge of rock with a drop of 3,000 feet on both sides. I was no fool: I dismounted and walked my horse across. Harding continued to ride. We took our time, but a third of the way across, I spoke his name quietly, not wanting to cause any unease to the horses.

Harding stopped then and looked back.

"Would you do me a great favor and dismount?"

He shrugged and got off his horse. I waited for him to make a wise crack about me being a packer and all, but it never came. I was glad of it.

We stopped halfway across, marveling at the scenery all around us. He pointed out the Utah Territory in the distance, a sight that I would always carry with me. At least once in their lifetime, everyone should see

Maggie's Way

such beauty from this eagle-eye perspective. Once across, Harding stopped and asked me, quite seriously, if I had been frightened for him.

"No, just worried about your horse." I grinned.

He did not smile and walked his horse on. I suppose I shouldn't have been so ornery, but a girl has to halt any romantic ideas if she doesn't want to be caught scrubbing floors and hushing babies.

The sky was clear with no threat of storms, so we continued on the Horsethief Trail. A half hour later, we broke for lunch — my treat this time, complete with cold fried chicken, rolls, and crisp green apples. While I spread out a small cotton cloth for our simple meal, Harding prodded absentmindedly at the ground with a fallen twig.

"Eat up, sir," I said.

He remained focused on the ground with no acknowledgment of my words.

"Not hungry, or afraid of my cooking?"

He worked steadily, stabbing at the dirt. I was about to accuse him of rudeness when he picked something up from the earth.

"Maggie, I've found a treasure." His eyes shone as bright as a harvest moon. He brushed dirt from the object. He then placed a worked piece of silver in my hand, filling the length of it.

"A Spanish cross!" I declared. I looked into his blue eyes and an unusual impression flooded over me. I had the distinct feeling this was a sign. My preacher was the genuine article, and I had nothing to fear.

27

DISCOVERIES

When not packing, I wandered throughout the hills. Although I admit I had more than a touch of prospector's fever, the splendor of the mountains enticed me. Now late in October, I felt compelled to roam the hillsides before the snow ushered in the long season of winter.

A wool coat under my oilcloth was now required, for the chill of changing seasons was upon us. The barren sky drew me further away, exploring a draw that was among the thousands in the San Juans I had never set eyes on. The deceptive sunlight made me confident in the warm autumn day, but every time I crossed under heavy trees, the chill gnawed at any exposed skin.

I rode along the bottom edge of a draw, studying the mottled rock wall. Then I stopped in my tracks. Smoke drifted up the side of a cliff wall. Friend or foe? I shifted in my saddle, looking around three-hundred-and-sixty degrees. Nothing was out of place, but an eerie silence greeted me. I sat quietly. Finally, I urged my horse forward. "Easy girl." Fifty feet from the smoke, I realized it wasn't smoke at all.

I dismounted, tied my horse to an aspen, and walked over. My hand dampened as it touched a wisp of steam jutting out of an opening in the rock. Entering the dark mouth of the cavern, I ducked my head. Beads of warm moisture formed on my face as I crept forward into the cave, navigating my way in the dim light. I counted on the fact that a wild animal would find this much too warm and humid for comfort.

Five feet back into the cavern, my head slammed against the lowered ceiling. The throbbing pain pulled me back outside. The cool air chilled me as the heavy moisture in my hair and clothing met the decreasing temperatures. Afraid of catching my death of cold, I untied Sierra and footslogged ahead of my horse. I hoped the physical motion would warm my blood and dry my clothing. Luckily, the wool in my inner coat warmed my body even while wet. After a mile of drying time, I remounted. On the ride back, I laughed out loud, my heart beating fast. I had found a vapor cave!

Back home, Ma soon had me sipping hot potato soup in the back kitchen. I was on my second bowl when a knock came at the door. I started to get up from the table, but Ma motioned me to remain seated.

"Who's calling?" she asked, not wanting to open the back door to a stranger after dark.

"It's Matthew, Ma'am," the familiar voice rang through the night air.

My spirits rose in anticipation of recounting my adventure so soon.

"Come in, Matthew, and have a bite to eat," Ma said.

"Good to see you, Mrs. O'Malley," Matthew said as he came in the door. "I've already had my dinner, but I wouldn't mind having a piece of your famous pie."

"Sit down, and I'll dish it right up."

Ma placed a hand on the back of his shoulder, directing him to the table. It was obvious she had grown fond of Matthew, always putting a good word in for him for my benefit. He gave me a quick wink and smile. I was itching to relate my latest discovery, but Ma was visiting with him.

"How has your day gone, Matthew?"

"Kept me going, it has. Performed one wedding, visited with two families with sickness, and talked to one husband I'd like to thrash."

"How's that?" Ma asked.

"I will not mention any names, but a man should either leave his wife alone or darn well help her if they are going to produce a whole litter of children, one right after another."

Even without names, I narrowed it down to one of two families. I watched Ma to see if his all-too-honest talk embarrassed her. It did not appear to, but I didn't feel like meeting his eyes just then.

He continued. "The poor woman hasn't a chance to recover between babies, and he never lifts a finger to help her when he's home."

I glanced at him between spoonfuls of soup then and saw his dark brows knit together and the corners of his mouth droop.

"Maggie's father, rest his soul, was a great help to me when she was born," Ma said. "When he had finished his job for the day, the first thing he did was grab Maggie and play with her so I could finish my chores." Ma excused herself then to see about the last customers of the day. My hunger stilled, and it was good timing. I was anxious to relate my finding. Matthew eyed another piece of pie, but, not forgetting his manners, he acknowledged me. His eyebrows lifted as he observed my eager face.

"So what are you dying to tell me, my Irish lass?"

With the conversation in my direction at last, I told the story of my adventure. Even before the second piece of pie was exhausted, his interest peaked. We talked on into the evening, until Ma subtly reminded us of the hour. Matthew bid us both good night and told me we would have to return to the cave before winter came on. I wholeheartedly agreed.

"Take care of that hard head of yours, Lassie," he said before he left.

I slung my napkin at him, but he ducked and raced out the back door. I could hear his laughter coming from outside and turned around to find Ma trying not to smile.

The next day, I passed a small group gathered around a man on the boardwalk. The talk was spirited, and, out of curiosity, I paused a few feet away. The man had long, scraggly hair hanging below a new wool hat. Ruddy cheeks rose in a perpetual smile beneath a drooping mustache as he talked. The face, in dreadful need of a good cleansing, contrasted with the man's new suit coat, vest, and freshly creased trousers — clothes more suited to a lawyer than a prospector. The eyes of all gathered were wide in awe as he related his discovery.

"I'm off to travel the world, I am," he claimed. "But first, boys, it's drinks on the house." A general cheer went up, and the small crowd entered the nearby saloon.

When I arrived at the stable, I told the story to Jonas.

"He sounds like one who'll go on a bender, spendin' and drinkin' all his fortune away," he said. "If he sells his claim for a substantial amount, it'll take him a while but, be sure, within a year or two his fortune will be gone. Then he'll probably be back prospectin' and livin' on beans an' bacon. After years of scrapin' by, sudden riches go to the head of most of these men. They don't 'ave a clue what to do with it 'cept spend it."

"Not me," I declared. "I would buy some land or cattle and do something grand with the money."

"You and I both," Jonas agreed. "But 'member, some of these men never did do an honest day's work for an honest day's pay. Others git carried away with the idea that for the first time in their life they can 'ford luxuries an' don't need to toil an' sweat just for the necessities of life. It makes 'em go a little loco."

As time went on, I learned the prospector made a moderate amount for his discovery, and the miner was paid well for his hard work; but the capitalist made out the best by selling stock in mines that often cost more than what they would produce. The investors from back East were usually the losers financially, especially in the San Juans, where the high cost of transporting the ore cut into the profits. Of course, there were those mines with such abundance of high-grade ore that the investment proved lucrative. Development here had been slow; not one capitalist had yet bought up a mine, though many saw that coming. So far, only small companies or capitalists had purchased and developed the mines.

The next week turned dreary as dropping temperatures spoke of winter's return. It was on such a morning that I walked to the stables. I had barely begun cleaning stalls and pitching hay than Dan, one of the stable hands, ran in shouting.

"Someone's hanging in a tree down by the river!" he said. He sucked in air, gasping for breath.

Jonas and another stable boy, Gus, hurried outside. I followed. Jonas turned back to me.

"Ya might not want ta' see this, gal."

I hesitated, but if this was happening in my town, I needed to know about it. I grabbed my coat off the hook. We all followed Dan as he jabbered about discovering the body on his way to work. He lived in a shack close to the river.

It was not a pretty sight, such an unnatural distortion of the human body. The dead man's back faced us, the head hanging at an odd angle. I looked away. Watching the faces of Jonas and the boys was almost as bad as they registered shock, revulsion, and, even worse with Gus, an almost delighted awe.

"Who is the unlucky sap?" asked Dan.

"It's the preacher man!" cried Gus.

My head jerked up to look at the swinging body again. The frame was too large and heavy for Matthew. I walked around to see the face. My heart pounded. Abercomby!

"Okay, boys, let's go back, and we'll report this to Mr. Dunnick. He'll know who to go to about this." Jonas motioned us back to the stable.

My head reeled. I made no sense of it. Dunnick stormed out of his office after Jonas told him the news. He mounted a horse and raced to notify William Munn, the town clerk. I was in shock during the hour we waited. When he returned, he related what he had learned. There had been a murder the previous night: a customer had killed one of the girls from the red light district. The young woman had been one of the miners' favorites. Reputedly, Abercomby was the customer who had viciously murdered her.

"Naw, it can't be," said Jonas. "He was a preacher . . . when these vigilantes get somethin' into der heads, innocent people die."

I looked over at Jonas, who stood shaking. I knew he was remembering the South, where hanging an innocent black man was common. I was the only one there who had good reason to believe what was being said of Abercomby could be true.

"Jonas," I whispered. "I'm going home."

His trembling arm escorted me out of the building.

"I knows you shouldn't 'ave seen that, gal."

However, it was not that alone. What had happened to that poor girl, prostitute or not, and the remembrance of that cold, ungodly look Abercomby had given me that time in the mountains had my mind and body churning.

"I'll walk ya home," he said.

"No, thanks. I'm okay."

I kept myself together until I knew Jonas had turned back. Then my stomach could no longer hold back all the poisonous venom connected to this day, and I retched over and over again.

28

UNCOMPAHGRE WATERS

Vigilante committees often took retribution, taking into their own hands situations that, in more established towns, were left to the law. Often warnings were given with anonymous letters declaring "Forewarned" and containing a drawing of a tree with a man hanging from it. The intention was to scare the offender out of town for good. In this case, however, the "soiled dove" had been popular with the local miners. Thoughts of mere warnings were not a consideration when a group of miners discovered her mutilated body.

The town clerk found some men, as the saying goes, to put Abercomby to bed with a pick and shovel. If only his afterlife would be that peaceful, for I knew a place of anguish was reserved for this man.

That evening I sent word to Jonas that I would miss work the next day. The following morning, I visited the hot springs near the river where the townspeople had damned up water in small pools. In the cold air, the steam rose thick like heavy fog over the warm water. The original name of the town, Uncompahgre, had originated from the Ute word for warm springs. I had been aiming to soak in the springs for some time and decided this was as good a time as any, seeing how most people would not come out in the cold, early morning. Taking off my boots and then lifting up my woolen dress worn specifically for this purpose, I lowered myself nigh up to my waist in the warm waters. Soothing, medicinal waters were what I needed. I wished it was further from town, hidden away in some draw where I could have stripped to my camisole and dipped up to my neck.

I heard footsteps approaching and whirled around, immediately thinking of my gun lying at the water's edge.

"It's only me, Maggie."

I was astounded to see Matthew.

"Your mother said she saw you walk off in this direction."

Then I became aware of my exposed camisole. I know my face turned crimson red. Matthew attempted to hide a smile.

"Turn your back, Matthew."

"Of course, but I'm going to soak too."

"Fine, as long as your back is turned."

"Just going to take my boots off."

In a moment, the water splashed as he stepped into the water.

"Are you okay?" he said.

"Fine."

"Good."

He did not say anything more for a while. "I'm going to stand next to you so you can lean against me."

What a ridiculous thing to do. Then I decided to take him up on it. I hadn't slept much last night. I leaned against his shoulder for support, as his arm stretched across my back. It felt good to have him so close, but even this thought I chased from my mind. I closed my eyes and thought about nothing but the warm, steamy water. I was grateful. For once, he didn't try to carry on a conversation. We were both soaking wet.

I smiled at the thought of how we would race back like children to avoid catching our death of a cold.

29

GUSTY GALES

My first taste of a San Juan winter came on the back of a late Indian summer. The packing trip up the mountain had been decent: partly cloudy but warm for the season. By mid-afternoon, the clouds obliterated the sun and solid gray filled the sky. A drizzle began. Halfway down the mountain, the rain changed to big, delightful flakes of snow. I felt as giddy as a child let out of school.

Within an hour it was another world altogether. The temperature dropped at least ten degrees, the mercury nearing the freezing point. The wind whistled up, and, to my misfortune, I was headed directly into the whirling gale, the snow no longer delightful but stinging my face.

The mules plodded on with heads low to keep the blinding snow from their eyes, faithfully continuing down the mountain with all the resignation of beasts of burden. The animals seemed to know their way back, despite the nonexistent field of vision; had it been up to me, we would have been in great trouble. What kept my reason was the fact that I could tell from how I sat in the saddle that we were still heading downhill, and, as long as we kept out of thick trees, I could rest assured we were still in the long ravine leading back to the valley. Still, I reminded myself of these facts to keep from panicking: becoming stranded in a blizzard was not a comfortable thought. The muffled peal of the bell from the last animal rang continually, reassuring me that my entire mule train was intact.

When I saw the edge of Ouray, lights were beginning to be lit. The days were becoming shorter, and the town was in constant shadow save for the few meager hours at midday. By the time I arrived at the stable at dusk, my face was numb. Jonas directed Dan to take care of the animals and led me to the wood stove at the rear of the building. I had felt warm enough riding. But once I was out of the wind and next to the radiating wood stove, I felt chilled all over, as if I was frozen and only now thawing out. My face began stinging with pain as it warmed near the heat. I decided then and there to always pack a wool scarf, extra pair of gloves, and additional socks in my saddlebags. Jonas walked me home against my protests. It seemed preposterous when I thought of the distance I had already traveled alone.

"I can't believe your ma ain't havin' a fit about this job ya 'ave taken on," Jonas said.

"She knows me too well," I responded. "People do what they want in the end, despite others good intentions."

"Reckon she's accepted that stubborn streak in ya by now."

In talking to one of the town board members, Amos learned that a census of sorts had to be compiled for the United States Land Office. So, in January with the new year of 1877 commencing, it was found that the town had a little over four hundred people living in it. This was misleading, for on the weekends it was more likely one thousand souls as the miners arrived to celebrate their time off from hard labor.

Amos carried out a brisk business and became more prosperous each day. He was a practical man, nevertheless, and put aside a good percentage in savings each month. He counseled Ma and me to do the same. The good thing about new mining towns was the quick money to be made, but ever looming was the real possibility that Ouray could become a ghost town if the ore ran thin or the market dropped. The high cost of extracting and freighting ore out of the mountains could pull the percentage of profit down to the point where it was not worth the cost of operation.

I had received a dollar and a half a day for stable work, but my wages had doubled to three dollars a day for packing. With my increased salary, I had money to save after paying Ma for room and board. I hoped the mining would hold out until I had enough saved for working some land or going into business for myself. I kept optimistic, since I'd hate to relocate and start over again. At this point, I wasn't sure what my business venture would entail, other than it would surely include animals. As for Amos's advice, the O'Malley women were way ahead of it.

30

WHISTLING WINDS

Two weatherworn prospectors looked up to see my mule train approaching on the narrow trail of the mountain ledge. They took the inside of the road, following the well-known rules of the trail. As the train approached, the brim of my slouch hat obscured my face. The blowing snow had me bent low over the saddle to keep the snow from my eyes. Some of the mules were loaded with wooden crates, so the first prospector swung his left leg over to the side to avoid a crushed leg.

"Ho, there," said the prospector upon passing.

"Hi, there," my higher voice rang.

The first prospector stopped his mule, craning his neck back. "Hey, Gus," he yelled over the wind.

I turned my head to see his buddy pull his horse up beside his partner.

"That there was the lady mule skinner we've heard 'bout."

I chuckled, as I continued down the trail, glad that I could find any humor on a day like this. The cold gnawed at the delicate patches of exposed skin around my eyes. The wool scarf wrapped around my face warded off frostbite. The high Rockies were not a hospitable place in the winter and certainly not for the fainthearted. Despite its harshness, it remained a place of strength and silent beauty for those with fortitude.

At first, I held my breath as the train met someone on a trail steep and narrow as this one, especially on a snow-covered path. Ultimately, I trusted the mules to avoid the edge. Normally, the lead mule's rope was wrapped around my saddle horn, but at these times, I undid the rope in case a mule would slip off the edge, taking the entire pack with him. I wanted neither my horse nor myself to follow that tragic route.

A gal with vanity would not have been caught dead dressed as I was. My body was a shapeless form due to the many layers of shirts and coats worn, but my sole concern was how to keep from freezing. Traversing uphill in snow made an interesting run with the mules. An animal would lunge forward to keep up with the mule ahead, another pulling back in the exertion of carrying a heavy load in the snow. I had to keep a strong grip on the rope wrapped around my saddle horn to insure I wouldn't lose it all in the back and forth commotion.

The mountains transformed into another creature altogether in the winter. At times the silence was overwhelming. The rocky peaks, many over fourteen thousand feet high, jutted out of the snow like the vertebrae of a giant behemoth. Some of the wildest, roughest terrain in the Rocky Mountain range was in the San Juans. I came out into the bowl beneath the great peaks just as it was becoming dark, the many small lights of Ouray shining promisingly in the distance. Arriving at Dunnick's, I handed the rope of the lead mule to a stable hand and led my horse into the warmth of the barn. Removing the saddle and gear as quickly as my half-numb hands would allow, I led Sierra into a stall with a well-deserved dinner of fresh hay and a pan of oats.

The stove blazed on this cold night. I remained only long enough to feel my skin sting as it slowly thawed. Eager for a warm meal and sleep, I made for home at a slow run. I pounded at the back door.

"Who is it?" an unfamiliar voice called out.

It had to be one of her workers.

"Maggie. Hey, it's cold out here," I said.

The door opened then, and I saw an unfamiliar face of a young woman. She was none too friendly and said nothing as she returned to her task of dishing up an order. Ma had evidently hired a new waitress. The kitchen was the best place to be on a night like this, other than the bed I longed to sink into. The blazing cookstove made the room toasty as the steam from a huge kettle of soup rose into the air like a welcome fog. I removed layer after layer of my clothing in the comforting heat. Ma walked in as I dipped up a big bowl of soup.

"Ah, Maggie," she said. "Home safe and sound." She gave me a quick hug and moved on to dishing up another customer's plate. I had arrived at the height of the dinner hour.

I downed my bowl of ham and bean soup along with two pieces of Ma's fine homemade bread. By the end of February, Ma had resigned herself to cooking only soups and stews. Winter turned hard with more snow than usual; shipments of supplies were becoming fewer and farther behind. Although Amos had forewarned Ma to stock up for the winter, even he had not foreseen its severity. It amazed me what Ma could create, as long as the flour, sugar, and beans held out. Soups, stews, and chili stretched the dwindling meat supply.

The new girl strolled into the kitchen as I was finishing up. She looked familiar, probably someone from Sunday services. Ma came back into the room. I kissed her good night, lit a candle, and climbed the narrow stairs to the second floor. So little heat escaped from the kitchen that it couldn't shake the frost, which glazed the open rafters. Not bothering to take the time to change to my nightgown in the chilling cold, I swept off my wool trousers and flannel shirt and snuggled under the many layers of quilts, clad in my long johns. The last thing I remembered was waiting for the heat of my body to warm the bed. I never heard the clang of pots and pans as they were washed and put away.

31

REVELATIONS

The gray dawn broke through the small window of the bedroom. I rose early, as I had fallen asleep at the premature hour of seven-thirty the night before. I had slept almost twelve hours. It was Sunday, and I had an agreement with Jonas that I would not work on the Sabbath so I could attend church services. I heard the banging of pots underneath the floor; Ma was up and about as usual. As I buttoned my shirt, I flinched when I glimpsed someone sleeping on the plank floor against the far wall. I crept closer to discover the young woman of the night before, wrapped in down-filled quilts. Her head rested upon a bunched up coat in lieu of a pillow. What was this about?

Downstairs Ma greeted me cheerily.

"Ma, who is that sleeping upstairs?"

"Her name is Lily. You went to bed so quickly I didn't get a chance to introduce my new worker." She poured me a cup of coffee along with one for herself and sat down at the table with me. O'Malley's didn't open until noon on Sunday, and it was the one morning Ma and I had to relax.

"But why is she sleeping here?"

"You know Cloe got married on the spur of the moment and left me at loose ends last week. Lily needed a job, and I needed to hire someone. Besides, she's been treated badly and has nowhere to go for the moment."

How could I argue with that? It felt awkward, though, to think this stranger would be living with us now.

"I remember when you were a babe, and I had nowhere to go; we were taken in by others. When I was able to repay Clara Brown for all her charity, she told me the best repayment was to pass the kindness on. I have never forgotten."

Though I said not a word, Ma had this uncanny knack of reading my thoughts. I was humbled by my lack of charity and stood reproved. More than likely, a carousing drinking miner had beat his young wife. Ma was right; the good Lord had blessed us in our move to Ouray. It was only right to pass some of it on. Halfway through our breakfast, the girl came downstairs.

"Good morning, Lily," Ma greeted the young woman. "How did you sleep?"

Maggie's Way

"Fine, Ma'am," she said.

She took the outstretched cup of coffee Ma held. With her dark hair caught back in a braid, the girl's pale, plain face revealed she was no older than sixteen.

"Lily, I would like you to meet my daughter, Maggie."

My mother exuded warmth that is hard to describe. Most people found her natural kindness hard to resist. Lily's bashful manner held, but a light came on in her eyes when Ma spoke to her. The girl acknowledged me with a brief nod, eyes diverted, and looked back at her coffee. I was having trouble deciding if she was dull or just plain shy. Ma dished a plate of hot cakes and side pork up for the girl. She tried to bring Lily into the conversation every so often, but the girl said very little and only responded to Ma with her eyes or a nod of her head. I wondered if this is what happened to people when they were mistreated.

A soft knock sounded at the back door. I looked up in surprise, wondering who it would be at this hour.

"I took it upon myself to invite Matthew for breakfast, since we have not seen him for a while," Ma said as she went to open the door.

I wondered if she was trying to influence matters, but I was eager to see him so I forgave her any ulterior intentions.

"Mrs. O'Malley, you're looking as lovely as ever," Matthew said.

"It is good to see you, Matthew, but compliments aren't necessary to get a good breakfast around here," she answered.

Ma was quite taken with Matthew. After all, he was a good, kind man. I pulled out a chair for him.

"Maggie, my girl, you're not a complete icicle then?"

His hand brushed mine as I held the chair back. I had missed the twinkle in those eyes more than I would admit. Ma soon had a full plate of cakes and side pork in front of Matthew.

"Lily, I warn you that you'll soon be adding pounds with Mrs. O'Malley's cooking," Matthew said.

"Her food is delicious." There was a slight accent about her voice.

Suddenly the girl could talk, and I noticed her countenance lit up with Matthew in the room. My guess must have been correct — one of his parishioners. A minute later, the girl hopped up and took the coffee off the stove.

"More coffee, Sir?" she asked. Her dull eyes burned bright now, a full-fledged smile spread across her face.

"I could use a warm-up. Thank you, Lily."

The girl flashed a big grin at him. What was her story? She stood by the table holding the coffee pot, as if waiting for Matthew to finish his freshly poured cup. She never cared to ask if I wanted more. Just then, Ma took the pot from her and suggested they set the tables for the dinner hour. She was giving us some time alone together, and I would appreciate it more without this strange girl interfering.

We had not seen each other for a few weeks, other than at Sunday services, and we were soon caught up in conversation. That week, Matthew told me, he held a funeral service for a miner. The young man had not accurately figured the time needed for a lit stick of dynamite to explode. Matthew was often called on to officiate, regardless of the fact that the person had not attended his services. It was expected of him as a preacher, though they often paid him a bit for it.

Time flew, and Matthew excused himself to set up the saloon for worship.

"I will see you at the service then, my Maggie girl," he said, with the same old half-mocking, half-flirting look I had grown accustomed to.

I felt the blood rush to my cheeks in response to his comment. After he left, I wondered if he thought of me as his girl, or was he only teasing? I could never be sure with Matthew. No sooner had he left than Ma and Lily returned to the kitchen. Ma announced it was time to dress for service.

"I'm going to stoke this fire first, Ma," I said.

I didn't wish to dress in front of a stranger, and, besides, it wouldn't take me long. After Lily descended the stairs, I went to get dressed. I smiled at her as she passed, but she pretended not to see. I put on my thick stockings and woolen dress; I redid my braid and curled a few tendrils around my face with my finger, my naturally wavy hair easily complying. When we were ready, Ma locked the door behind us. We hurried down the street to the service, eager to be out of the cold. Matthew stood at the door, greeting everyone upon arrival.

"Good to see you again this morning, Lily."

Lily smiled coquettishly at Matthew and turned back to look at me. That haughty look was one I had seen before, and I recognized the young woman at last. It was the girl at the house of ill repute!

"Don't I get a smile there, girl?" Matthew said to me. He placed a hand on my shoulder to get my attention.

"Oh . . . hello, Matthew," I said.

I looked back at Ma, incredulous that she had not told me who Lily was. Perhaps she didn't know. Well, this was not the time or place. We all sat down in the second row of chairs. I glanced over at Lily, who looked as prim as any church mouse. Her demeanor appeared as if she sat here every Sunday. Who knew if this girl could be trusted? My mind churned and boiled over, making it more difficult for me to sit still. It was the longest service I ever remembered, and I could not recall one thought of it. I watched to see if anyone was staring at us, but no one seemed concerned. Without her fancy dress and painted face, people did not detect the truth.

Later when Ma was preparing for the lunch hour, I knew I had to talk to her. As Lily scuttled back and forth placing bread and butter on the tables, I managed to get my question in.

"Ma, why didn't you tell me the whole story with Lily?"

"Lower your voice, Maggie," she said. "I wanted to give her a chance before you judged her."

"How do you know she won't rob you blind?" I said.

"I suppose there's no guarantee, but the girl has been abused by both her customers and her madam. She is all alone and deserves a chance. Anyway, you know I don't keep more than a day's worth of money here. The rest is in Amos's safe." Ma looked at me gently with the confidence of a woman who knows exactly what she is doing.

"I hope you won't come to regret this."

"I've offered her room and board for a few months until she gets some money saved. I'm only giving her a square chance at a better life, Maggie."

It sounded charitable and fair, leaving me without any further argument. However, I still held my reservations, and I intended to keep them.

32

DIAMONDS IN THE SNOW

The snow coruscated under the bright sky, the light refracting like miniscule diamonds, sparkling and winking under the sunshine. I was
descending the mountainside on a long journey down from Porter's on
this March day. It was of paramount importance that the mules did not
stray from the trail for danger of floundering in deep snow. I packed a
shovel but ever prayed that it would not be required. It would be a chore
to free an animal by myself.

I was on the last leg of the trip with miles to go. The mule train
advanced on the Waterhole slide area, where frequent avalanches
erupted and snow accumulated up to thirty feet or more. Steep snow-
banks ascended on each side of the trail, parallel to the top of a man's hat
as he rode horseback. The trail ran over deeply packed snow, as there had
been a slide here the month before. I dreaded traveling it: The walls on
each side brought sudden visions of a frosty burial. On the way up, a
queasy feeling surged through me as I passed it, and I quite expected to
feel the same coming down.

The cheery sunshine alleviated my fears, as the train proceeded
through the high-banked trail uneventfully. I felt relief when I saw the
last mule clear the area and come out where the banks were back to two
feet high.

No sooner had I turned around to face the trail when I heard a
tremendous roar. Instinctively, I kicked my horse's side and urged the
pack train faster. A rushing sound louder than any freight train threatened to deafen my ears, booming a thunderous noise I would not soon
forget. As I impelled my horse on, I turned to see snow rising in the air
like a great cloud, gathering in intensity as it transcended the steep
slope and gaining in magnitude every second. My eyes unable to leave
the sight, I watched as the slide rushed to the spot where we had been
only moments before, the Herculean force throwing thick trunks of
trees and great boulders as if they were mere feathers . . . plunging,
tumbling, crashing, pitching, toppling in the most powerful force of
nature I was ever to witness. Soon the disturbed snow billowed high
into the air, obscuring the area from sight. The animals frothed and

panted. I realized then that they had needed no prompting to rush from the area.

I managed to stop the mules within a fifth of a mile. Curiosity took complete control of me, and I managed to tie my horse to a tree branch in arm's reach from the trail, no small feat since I instantly sunk to my waist in the process. This taken care of, I walked back to the site of the avalanche flow.

An unearthly silence enveloped me in the aftermath, the only sound my pounding heart. I looked up at the snow, which now stood forty feet above the level it was a few minutes before. It had packed rock and timber debris into the banks, and they poked out at odd places. I stood there for several minutes with the furious movement replaying itself over again in my mind, while the roar echoed in my ears despite the pervading stillness.

The silence was unnatural and downright spooky, as if the world had stopped in its tracks. I returned to the comfort of the animals. As I walked, I recalled how often Jonas had warned me about avalanches. As a rule, it rarely became as cold here as it did back East, and that very fact contributed to the avalanche danger. The large amount of heavy moisture-filled snow, combined with warm weather and the steep slopes of the San Juans, made for a lethal combination. I reached the mule train and remounted my nervous horse, finishing the ride back as I pondered how my life could have easily ended. I considered the most important things in my life. Two names pressed heavily on my mind — my dear mother and a special man named Matthew.

My reservations concerning Lily lingered, but I tried to be amiable. She was often churlish and when not that, sullen. She had a definite lean toward gossip; I often heard her long-tongued stories about various customers spewed out to other workers. I fought the resentment surfacing in full force for her many unattractive traits.

One morning not long after she had come to stay with us, I had forgotten my hat and bounded up the stairs to retrieve it. I intruded upon Lily changing from her nightgown to her work dress. Ugly bruises covered her upper arms and below her collarbone. They were turning that sickly shade of green that only deep bruises can. I pretended not to see, and I know I embarrassed her, coming upon her wounds like that. After that, I worked harder to suppress my feelings of irritation and resentment. I had prayed about my feelings toward her, knowing they were not very charitable. I believe I received an answer the day I began to think of Lily's situation not unlike the many abused mules I had witnessed. It was not the animal's fault that its temperament went sour, sometimes even explosive. It was a natural reaction to cruelty. This helped me considerably at those times the haughty look was directed at me. In addition, we had no idea what had happened in her youth to push her into the detestable life of the harlot. Yet I knew people with the hardest of circumstances who managed to lift themselves above the squalor. Human nature was an unpredictable thing: some broke from tragedy, some succumbed to lowness, while others managed to rise above it.

One afternoon a week later, I was finishing up the stalls. The sun sank below the peaks, typical of this time of the year. I stood just outside the stable doors, taking in a welcome breath of fresh air after the swirling hay dust. A column of horses and mules rode up the muddy street in front of Dunnick's. The riders' heads hung low, weary and tired from a long journey. As they passed the stable, I saw packs on the backs of the mules. A boot poking out beneath a canvas cover revealed no common freight. The same odd shape draped over all five mules. My rapt face watched as a young man bringing up the rear rode over to me. Up close, I saw the fear that remained on his exhausted, sunburned face.

"Took us most of yesterday trying to dig out any possible survivors. Only thing that made it was a young mule, but turned out his leg was broke so had to put him under. Do you know a preacher about this way?"

"I do. Lives just down a ways with a family in the first log cabin to the east. His name is Matthew Harding."

"Thank you." He trotted his horse to catch up with the solemn parade.

Jonas strode up to me then, looking after the departing train of men. "Avalanche?"

"The mountain got five of them," I said, still staring after them.

He said nothing more but patted my shoulder before walking inside. I figured he was blaming himself for helping me get into this business, but, just then, I didn't feel up to assuaging his guilt. My mind drifted once again to what I wanted my life to be about — that is, if it lasted long enough.

Maggie's Way

A Snow-slide in the Rocky Mountains —
drawn by Charles Graham.
Harper's Weekly February 17, 1883

33

SPRINGTIME IN THE ROCKIES

The arrival of spring brought high rushing streams and riverbanks brimming from the constantly thawing snow. After the town lost most of its snow, it contended with the aftermath — mud. In contrast, high on the peaks the remaining snow still shone brightly. It would be late June before most of that disappeared. Now in late May, Matthew and I were finally off on our long-awaited trip to the vapor cave I had discovered the previous autumn.

We had picked a good day for our journey and left early as usual. This time I came prepared, bringing phosphorus matches and a torch made of oil-soaked cloth wrapped around a thick branch. I suggested we both bring extra clothing, recalling the chill I had gotten last time from the drenching steam. No doubt about it, we were both excited about exploring the cave.

By midmorning, we had arrived at the mouth of the cave and secured our horses nearby. Matthew lit the torch and gave me — as the discoverer of the cave — the privilege of entering first. I warned him our exploration might include a lot of bending and possibly crawling, if warranted. Ducking our heads as we entered, the light revealed multiple colors of dripping minerals and crystals shining like jewels. Then, as I feared, we were soon crouching down. My back ached from the strain of stooping as we crept through the narrowing crevice. The passage opened up then into a small room, where we were able to stand to our full height. Matthew's face shone with excitement. He took the torch and walked around investigating the cavern. Disappointedly, we found no further passages reaching into the mountainside. I sat on a low ledge and looked around the small vapor cave. Matthew joined me, and we marveled at the multicolored stalagmites hanging all about us.

At last, Matthew spoke. "So, my Irish lass, do you envision any adventures other than mule skinning?"

"I have considered some new ventures," I answered.

"Such as?"

"Homesteading . . . raising cattle, perhaps. Miners have to eat, so there would always be a ready market. It would give me opportunities to ride the hills and still leave some time to prospect now and then." I looked up at him with a confident smile.

"You sound like a practical businesswoman: common sense with a love of adventure. My kind of woman." He paused. "Do you think you might ever settle down with one man for a lifetime?"

Out of the corner of my eye, I noticed his gaze fixed on the opposite wall of the cave.

"I suppose I might consider it if it made good business sense," I said, with a mocking tone, "and if it was a binding legal arrangement, of course."

"Do you think a preacher would fit into your plans there somewhere?"

His eyes remained focused straight ahead, avoiding mine. I had learned from experience not to tread carelessly on his feelings.

"I suppose cows need prayer, too." I enjoyed teasing him.

Then at last he looked at me.

"What would you think of hitching up with me?" His face looked as solemn as if he were conducting one of his funerals.

"I would consider it, if I was asked." I was relentless.

"Well, lass, I *am* asking. Would you marry me, Maggie O'Malley?"

I looked up at the face that had become so dear to me. My heart melted as I saw his eyes shine with too much moisture, the brows knit together in uncertainty. Was he remembering all too well the proud, independent Maggie who thought she did not need anyone in her life?

I reached for his hand. "I would be proud to marry you, Matthew Harding."

There in the heavy damp air of the cave among the magnificent stalagmites, we kissed for the third time. With this prospecting preacher man, I figured I would strike gold on both sides — here and the hereafter!

34

RECONSIDERATION

The dark emotion of fear bore down upon me the next morning, for thinking all my adventures might be finished. In the morning's light, the monumental decision I had made appeared too hastily decided. To complicate matters, in the excitement of the moment, Matthew and I had told Ma, who was happier than a bluebird on the first day of spring.

Unable to admit my feelings to her, I went riding. I kept to the south-facing hills, where the sun's rays reached and dried the slopes. I rode at a fast clip through the forest, dodging in and out of trees. Thoughts flew through my head. Had I relegated myself to the specter of an apron-bound wife? Would raising cattle become Matthew's job solely, while I sat in a small cabin waiting? How well did I know this man after all?

When I returned in the late afternoon, I headed straight to the Forman house where Matthew kept a room. I had to talk to him right away.

He was not in. I left a message that he contact me as soon as he returned. Back home, I feigned illness and retreated to the upstairs in privacy. I read a book while I waited, glad to escape in an adventurous novel, which served to reinforce my desire not to lose this part of my life. After a couple of anxious hours waiting for Matthew, I went down to the kitchen to claim a quick recovery and a meal. Just as I was descending the stairs, I heard Lily report my ill health to someone at the door. I rushed out to see Matthew walking away.

"Matthew," I yelled. "I need to talk to you."

I turned back to see Lily's surveillance at the door, and I stared at her until she closed it at last. Matthew walked up to me — his steps measured and deliberate, his face intent on the ground, his eyes making no contact with mine. I wondered if he harbored his own doubts. He attempted a weak, unnatural smile.

"So have you reconsidered already, Maggie?"

A somber look glazed his face. How could he know how I felt?

"I want to talk to you," I said.

"So you said."

I could not stand looking at his face, devoid of emotion.

Maggie's Way

"We can talk down by the river," I suggested.

We walked in silence, but not in comfort. How could I tell the man I loved the fears I held of a life together?

We arrived at the riverbank.

"Matthew . . ."

"Yes?"

"I am afraid I would not be what you want in a wife. Marriage will not turn me into the perfect preacher's wife content to stay home the rest of my life." I studied the ground beneath my feet.

I did not want to lose him . . . yet, I could not be other than who I was.

I did not want to hurt him.

"I didn't ask you to be a preacher's wife. I asked you to be *my* wife."

"I can't be something I am not," I insisted. This time I looked him straight in the eyes.

"I love *you*, Maggie, not some idealized picture of a wife you seem to think I have. If I was looking for someone like that I would have found her by now. I fell in love with a trouser-wearing, mule-skinning woman with all the stubbornness of Ireland, and, believe me, I have no illusions of you as anything else."

I drew nearer to him then, but he pulled away. What was this I detected? His taut face exposed the strong angles of his jaw and cheek-bones, his eyes shone cold without the familiar laugh lines to lift his eyes, his brows drew down as in distaste of something repulsive. This anger was something I had never seen before.

"I didn't realize you knew me so little as to think I would box you into something you didn't want or treat you with anything other than respect." His brows knitted together, his face tight with anger. "And another thing, Miss Maggie O'Malley, I have never asked another woman to marry me before, and I take that very seriously. If you aren't able to commit your life to me as I intend with you, then you'd better tell me right now."

I had never seen him so stern, but he was right. If I thought he was the type of man I could not live with, I had no right to encourage him. But all I had ever seen from him was kindness and humor — never any undue expectations of me.

"I'm sorry, Matthew. I began to get these awful visions of never stepping outside the four walls of a cabin. I became afraid that you would try to change me."

"That would be like waiting for hell to freeze over, gal," he said. "So do you love me or not?"

"You know I do."

He broke out in a grin, and never was I more eager to see it. Matthew walked over to me at last and held me.

"When do you want to get married, O'Malley?"

"As soon as it is reasonable, and before I get cold feet again."

"Then it will be as soon as possible." He picked me up and gave me a great bear hug. Then we walked back to the restaurant.

"Go and tell Ma the wedding's still on," he said, smiling as he left me at the door.

I had underestimated him. I could see that one of my life's adventures would be taking a lifetime to get to know this man in greater depth. We set the day for the wedding on June 25, which gave us a month to make our plans.

Matthew had heard talk of the latest prospecting hot spot discovered by Colonel S. H. Baker just over the Dallas Divide. What was so appealing to us was that this discovery was near lush meadows intertwined in the foothills — perfect for raising cattle. Our future plans included purchasing a wood stove and a canvas tent to serve as a temporary abode. We would construct a cabin through the summer and into the early fall. Together, we had adequate savings put aside for stock animals and provisions for the winter.

Matthew expected a boom in the area and figured there would be a call for preaching. In the meantime, he would have his hands full with building a cabin and a small holding pen for calves. His congregation in Ouray talked him into returning once a month for a service. It was a perfect solution, not only for the church, but also for visiting Ma. I was troubled about leaving her, but she insisted a couple had to have some privacy in their first years together. She was certain she could talk Amos into regular trips in his buckboard to visit us. I tried to avoid thinking about not seeing Ma on a daily basis, but I knew she was right about a couple needing time to settle into their new life.

35

LAST TRIP

Heading up the mountain on my last pack trip, the peaks circled the Ouray amphitheater like many points on a royal crown. A mixture of melancholy, awe, and gratitude for being able to see so much of these mysterious and beautiful mountains suddenly filled my heart.

By June twentieth, the lower elevations were free of snow, but isolated banks still persisted above timberline. The irony of this last trip was the fact that this was one of the roughest trails I would ever encounter. I was heading a fifteen-burro expedition up to the Grizzly Bear Mine. The rich silver operation, located several miles up Bear Creek in a remote, nearly inaccessible area, had been discovered two years earlier. I admit I felt trepidation about the trip, as the narrow trail had a reputation for being extremely dangerous. Jonas made sure I packed burros this time.

The journey began on an old Indian pathway. The sun was out in force, and I hoped it would melt any ice left on the north-facing slope. Glancing down the steep precipice of the Uncompahgre Gorge, I found we were still climbing. The uppermost branches of pines looked tiny; the massive trees were rooted far below. I had never seen the likes of such a drop.

"God's mercies," I said. I whistled at the sight, the sound echoing over the slopes like a ghost wailing. Sierra nickered, anxious to continue the journey, her eyes wide and alert. I broke out in a sweat, despite the fact that the sun had not yet taken the chill off the mountains. I dismounted in order to keep my nerve. Even so, I came to the point where I could no longer stand to look down at the canyon floor five hundred feet below.

The miners had not embellished the tale of this narrow trail; a jeopardous drop was often a foot away from its edge. I looked at the next step my foot would take, trying not to think about the man who had fallen to his death two weeks earlier, slipping down the cliff during a rain storm. I had judiciously never spoken of the incident to Ma or Matthew. Although Ma never scolded me again after our initial argument about my job, I knew she worried as mothers are prone to do. In regard to Matthew, I was keeping this as a trump card for the future, in case he ever doubted my abilities.

As I led Sierra with a lead rope I kept for such purposes, a sudden nudge at my back propelled me across the slick trail. Down I went, not knowing what had happened. My legs dangled over the edge — my hands clinging to the dirt, my right hand slipping over ice. I hung frozen for a moment, knowing if I continued to slide, I would end up like the miner in the rainstorm. Slowly, I swung my left leg over onto the trail, balancing my body ever so precisely throughout the motion. I moved little by little — my life depended on it.

I got both of my legs back on the trail and rolled away from the edge, as quickly as a squirrel chased up a tree. I jumped to my feet and glared at Sierra, who was several feet ahead. The nudge was her way of asking for a sugar cube, but it had nearly cost me my life!

My burros and I trudged on to our destination. I shivered as cool air swept over me, my clothing still damp from the sweat of hot fear. I gave up leading Sierra and instead drove her, along with the burros, from the rear. I no longer walked in the trail's center, instead, I hugged the inside edge. Then a loud thud sounded ahead: a burro had fallen to the ground and was flailing on the rim as I had been only moments before. My hands grasped my face in horror as I continued to watch. The animal struggled but managed to catch its feet and right itself. My heart wedged in my throat; I thought what an irony it was that my last packing trip also proved to be the most perilous of all my adventures.

I said a prayer of gratitude when I cleared the top and continued on the last leg of the journey. I took Jonas's sage advice to stay the night at the mining camp, for I dared not risk the wet spots on the trail turning into ice, as the sun dropped and temperatures plummeted.

It was June twenty-fifth. Fifty or so family and friends gathered in a meadow of wildflowers beneath a quiet mountain slope. The town of Ouray lay hidden below the forested hill, yet the site was only a short ride from town. Matthew's congregation had come out in full force. It was not every day your preacher got married. The assembly gathered in a small clearing with luminous aspen clustered among stately pines. Ribbons tied to several trees gave a festive air to our outdoor chapel. Fred Appleton, one of the church fathers, stood waiting to do the honors for the ceremony.

Matthew talked with some of the men on one edge of the clearing, while I remained with Ma and several matrons on the opposite side. I wore the linen and lace dress that Ma had worn years ago for her own wedding. She added a layer of lace at the bottom hem to make up for my longer legs. My dark auburn hair was upswept on the sides with the back cascading down. She tucked a few stalks of wild iris in my hair on one side. With everyone waiting for the ceremony to begin, I fidgeted. "Do you think I'll make him happy?" I whispered to Ma. I watched Matthew in the distance, straightening his collar.

"Maggie, darling," she said. "The fact that you're concerned about him ensures you'll make him happy." She wrapped her arms around me, the fragrance of lavender rising from her wrists. "There's a lot in life to fear, but don't be afraid to be happy, Maggie."

Mabel Hawkins pulled a bouquet of wildflowers from an enamel pitcher of water and wrapped the stems with a white cloth. As they were placed in my hands, I glanced over to see Matthew shuffling nervously as he spoke to one of the men. Marv Hansen began to play an Irish tune on his fiddle, the sign that the ceremony was beginning.

Ma kissed me with a tear in her eye and directed me over to Amos and Jonas. Amos smelled of bayberry cologne. He kissed my hand before folding my arm over his. "You'll do fine," he said. Whether regarding the ceremony or marriage, I wasn't clear. I smiled at Jonas and linked my other arm with his. He nodded at me — poor Jonas was almost as nervous as I was.

To maintain my composure, I didn't watch the crowd, but kept my eyes on Matthew. He winked, knowing it would make me smile. I took a deep breath and felt my shoulders relax. With one man on each side, my good friends escorted me down the "aisle" made from a long runner of cloth.

The music ended soon after I joined Matthew. We stood in front of Fred, who beamed with pride for the role he played that day. I tried to listen closely to his carefully chosen words, but I admit I missed most of them. I heard the part about two becoming one and about loving, respecting, and honoring each other. I knew my life was changing in ways I could not fully comprehend at the time, but I was convinced that Matthew was the kind of man I could submit to with full confidence. I looked into those gentle eyes. If I had not believed what I saw there, I'd have leaped on my horse and raced away.

Fred announced us husband and wife, and the crowd cheered. Matthew grasped me around the waist, spun me around, then kissed me like a star bursting.

When I opened my eyes, Ma stood nearby with tears of joy shimmering in her eyes. She encircled us in one big hug. "Congratulations," she said. "God bless you with a long life together." I'm sure her tears spoke also of sadness for the transition that was about to begin in both our lives.

"We'll expect frequent visits from you, Mother O'Malley," Matthew said, "and, of course, we'll be stopping in for your good cooking whenever we're in town." Amos and Jonas shook our hands, and then the crowd was upon us, eager to personally give their congratulations.

With the amenities at last fulfilled, the fiddle playing started up, accompanied by a harmonica and jug blowing. Some of the women spread blankets on the ground, while others set the picnic food on wooden boxes that were placed together as an impromptu table.

We were blessed by a beautiful day. The amiable climate was fortunate, for I had threatened to postpone the ceremony for ill weather. After two hours of socializing, Matthew insisted we leave the revelers in order to make the trip near Dallas Divide before dark. I said goodbye to Ma, both of us now in tears.

Our packed wagon awaited us in town. The two mules we had purchased were hitched up and awaiting our departure. We tied our horses to the back of the wagon. Traveling down the road with my new husband, I felt a strange mixture of excitement, melancholy, and anxiety. I was headed toward a new life, and, like moving to a foreign country, I hardly knew the language.

Maggie's Way

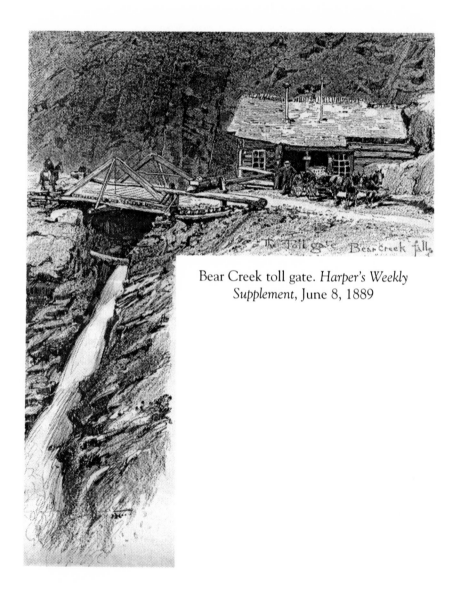

Bear Creek toll gate. *Harper's Weekly Supplement*, June 8, 1889

36

DALLAS DIVIDE

B y evening, we had crossed Dallas Divide and stopped halfway between the Divide and the new settlement of Placerville, named for the placer gold discovered there. When we came upon the rolling grass hills of our homesteading plot, we knew this was indeed a good place for cattle. We stopped for the night and set out our bedrolls, side by side. I tugged at my boots as I sat on my bedding, suddenly feeling like an unprepared student being asked to recite her lessons. I was a married woman now. Matthew stretched out on top of his woolen blanket, hands clasped behind his head.

"Maggie," he said. "Let's watch for shooting stars."

I followed his example and, reclining on my back, scanned the glittery sky. I was glad for the diversion. He pointed out the Big Dipper and the North Star, which of course I fully recognized but didn't say so. The night air rolled over us, crisp and piney-sweet. We watched for a long time until I finally caught the first falling star out of the corner of my eye. After a while, I began to think my husband would fall asleep — on our wedding night, no less. At last, my anxiety disappeared, and I rolled over to snuggle up to him. His hands remained behind his head, the starlight falling over his face, soft like gentle dew.

"Matthew Harding," I said, at last. "Are you going to kiss me or not?"

He broke out laughing and then swooped me up in his strong arms. We eventually slept like babes under the twinkling stars.

The next day I woke to the sweet song of meadow birds, as my head rested on the shoulder of my husband. It was a beautiful morning. I was grateful for the muffins and bread Ma had packed for us the day before, as it kept us from unpacking the wagon to prepare a proper breakfast. After eating, we were eager to find a spot where we would build our cabin. We drove the wagon to the base of the timbered hills, tied up the mules after we unhitched them from the wagon, and rode our horses to scout for the best location.

I spotted aspen intermingled with pines near a babbling creek and knew this was where I wanted the cabin. The hills obscured the distant trail below that led to Placerville. When he returned, Matthew agreed the proximity to water and forested hills was ideal. I knew he was

Maggie's Way

considering the availability of game animals and the promise of minerals above. I stayed while he rode back for the wagon. By climbing to a nearby rise, I saw the lower valley below, and above me the high peaks. It made sense to build here. When Matthew returned, he revealed his reservations about my site for the cabin. He didn't want to build in a blind pocket; he wanted to be able to see any travelers approaching. Just a short way over the hill was such a site.

That first day, we assembled our canvas tent and set up camp, not knowing when the next mountain shower would occur. Rain was common in the high country. On the second day, we started our building project. Matthew cut pine from the nearby hills while I cooked an Irish stew in a large kettle, adding some dried meat to the potato, carrots, and onion medley. Thus, I figured my cooking would be taken care of, other than adding fuel to the fire and giving a quick stir now and then. It would free me to help Matthew fell the trees.

We worked the two-man saw until Matthew judged the tree was ready. Next, we tied one of the mules to the end of a long rope attached to the trunk. After securing the rope, Matthew stopped to wipe the sweat from his brow and take a breath.

"I've given our mules names," I informed him.

"Is that right? He smiled at me as he leaned against an uncut tree. "And whatever could those names be?"

"Mo and Joe," I said. "Short and matching. What do you think?"

"Easy enough to remember, I suppose."

"Brought you a jug of cool water."

After taking his fill of the sweet spring water, Matthew's arm caught me around the waist and drew me to him. This was one advantage of living away from town: I could have my fill of kisses and embraces throughout the day.

I had purchased Mo and Joe from Dunnick's at a ridiculously low price. I had selected mules that had packed for several years, purposefully choosing two with obvious sores that never quite healed from constant packing. I knew that away from freighting they would recover, granted, with scars, but the otherwise strong, healthy animals would be useful in working our homestead.

One thing I would not miss from my freighting days was witnessing the abuse the animals were subjected to. Working for Dunnick's, I had no choice in the weight of the load packed on the animal's back. Dunnick's motivation was profit, and that meant packing as much supplies and ore as possible. Although a pad was used under the cross saddle, most mules

Maggie's Way

had back sores from the constant irritation of the daily load. I was glad to save at least two animals from a lifetime of misery. Although we would put them to work, from the mule's point of view, it was going to seem like heaven in comparison with commercial packing.

Matthew and I continued to cut the thick pine trunks. After a bit, I went to check the fire under the stew pot. Satisfied that it was going well, I returned to the timber-covered hillside. I arrived just as Matthew led Joe away from the tree to which he was tied with a stout rope. He encouraged him with a small switch on the rump. I laughed at the sight, remembering how much more this animal had endured at the hand of a cruel mule skinner. Within a few minutes, the sound of cracking wood rang out. Matthew let loose of the rope while prodding the mule into a run, ensuring Joe was out of reach from the falling tree.

On the first day of our building project, we finished up with seven good lengths of neatly trimmed, thick logs. After that, we grew more efficient and managed to fell and trim twelve trees per day, stopping only for a brief lunch. We worked diligently, knowing the summer season was fleeting and our cabin needed to be ready by fall.

Each day started with an early breakfast at dawn. A routine began that very first day that continued throughout our marriage. After finishing our meal, Matthew would read aloud from Psalms as we had our coffee. Then he reached for my hand, and we offered the day to our heavenly Father and asked for His blessings upon it. As I cleaned up the breakfast dishes, Matthew would head up the hill to check on the animals. He never started his morning chores without first kissing me goodbye. This pattern did not sputter out like sparks from a dying campfire; it became ingrained into our life together.

The days flew by with the sheer exhaustion of hard physical work and the delight of sharing each day together, but by late afternoon or early evening I often found myself missing Ma. Eventually, I realized this was about the time I used to return home from work. Matthew planned to return to Ouray in three weeks, and I could hardly wait. Other than loneliness from missing Ma, I found no regrets in my new life with Matthew.

We were happy as two lovebirds, spending all our time together. I felt lucky to have such a handsome husband, and one that was so kind and considerate. He was my best friend, and I his. Our mutual respect for one another proved our love a lasting one, although time would reveal our many differences.

Maggie's Way

37

COYOTE SONGS

The last light of day hovered as Matthew set down a thick bundle of fallen branches and small logs. I built up the campfire with some of the wood. As the dark settled upon us, I prepared a pot of hot tea after a day of strenuous work. After the water came to a rollicking boil, I added loose tea to the pot and took it off the flame to steep. I relished this time of day when we would relax after being so busy. Occasionally, a birdcall off in the distance broke the silence. A cool breeze swept over my face, pressing me near the warmth of the campfire.

"I think we have enough lumber to build our cabin, Maggie," Matthew said.

I poured him a cup of steaming tea and one for myself.

"I'm glad to hear that. I will admit, it has become a monotonous chore."

"I thought we would head up to Ouray tomorrow, spend a few days with Ma O'Malley. I'll hold a service on Sunday as promised and recruit enough people to come over next weekend to raise our cabin."

"It'll be nice to see other than just your mug for a change," I teased.

"Tired of me already?" he said.

"Not quite yet, but I'm looking forward to seeing Ma. Besides, we need to stock up on food staples while we're there."

"I'm afraid it will be a busy few months for us, Maggie. We have a lot to do. Once our cabin is up, I'll be much relieved. I promise we'll take a break then."

I didn't say anything in complaint, but, truth be said, I was more than ready for a respite from our toil. We sat in silence, enjoying the tranquility of the evening. After our second cup of tea, I contemplated turning in when the wild yip of a coyote rang out on the still, crisp night air. Several more wild voices answered over the hills. A coyote and her pups must be in the area. By the sound of it, they were far enough away to serenade us to sleep. Later, I drifted off, dreaming of the wild creatures sharing our world.

✧ ✧ ✧

We rode into town with the entourage of our two horses, with Mo and Joe following on leads. We could not leave our mules behind without neighbors to watch them, so, like children, they had to accompany us. Ma had no idea we were arriving and would certainly be surprised. We picketed the animals behind the restaurant, the long grass in need of cropping anyway. I tried the back door and, finding it unlocked, opened it to an unoccupied room.

I poured two cups of coffee for us and waited for Ma to dash back at any moment to dish up more food. A quarter of a cup down, the door swung open. True enough, it was Ma whose eyes widened as she stopped in midstep. I got up then to give her a hug. I felt warm moisture on my cheek. Could my strong mother be crying? Soon my own tears were mixing with hers. It was quite a reunion with all the crying and laughing going on.

"You'd think that we had been gone three years instead of three weeks," Matthew said at last.

"Young man, you come over here and get your hug too," Ma said.

Matthew embraced her.

"I have been taking good care of her, Mother O'Malley."

"Of that I have no doubt, but is she taking care of you?"

"That she is, Ma'am. Better than I expected." Matthew turned to give me a wink.

We enjoyed a full dinner of Ma's hearty roast beef with all the trimmings. I swear Matthew had three servings. He was so full that we held off on pie until later. We had a good time catching up on the local happenings. The most surprising news of all was Lily's engagement to one of the young men that took my place at Dunnick's. I was happy to hear it, because, I admit, I still did not quite trust her. Perhaps that was wrong of me, but I was protective of Ma and worried about anyone taking advantage of her. Matthew always said that should be the last of my worries. He joked he would never worry about strong-willed Irish women.

I made a point of visiting Amos and Jonas, each of whom was the closest I had to a father. When Amos mentioned he needed to hire someone to help at his store, I put in a good word for Jonas. I was happy to hear later that he had hired him. Jonas deserved to have a job with less physical strain, and Amos told me he was the best help he ever had. Over time, they became great friends, which pleased me to no end.

Maggie's Way

Matthew and I got up early the next morning and took a dip in the hot springs. We watched the sky ignite with orange and mauve-shadowed clouds on the high horizon. I thought about how much my life had changed since I was here last; I shook the nagging feeling that it would consist of nothing but cooking and cutting wood. I reminded myself that the day would soon arrive when we could plan our cattle enterprise.

During the service at the Bucket of Blood Saloon, Matthew asked for volunteers to raise our cabin in lieu of the offering. Every man raised his hand in answer, and it was a real testimony to see how well respected my husband was. I realized how fortunate I was to have found a man of his caliber. Ma stood and volunteered to cook barbecue beef for all, if each family would bring a dish to pass. I hoped that we would come to know good people like this in the Placerville area.

A huge party gathered at our place a week later. They began to arrive Saturday morning and kept coming into the early afternoon. Our quiet mountainside retreat was transformed to a community in itself. Entire families came, so there were children running around while the women attended to cooking and the men did the hard work of building. They notched the ends of the logs we had collected and began forming the walls of our cabin.

Despite the incredible amount of food, it kept disappearing. The women continually refilled empty bowls and added more entrees to the end of the wagons we used as impromptu buffets. The men and children ate in spurts throughout the day, the men needing fuel for the hard physical labor expended. The variety of dishes that made up the potluck created a true feast, and all enjoyed Ma's barbecue beef.

The long summer day proved valuable as the men worked into the evening, finishing up the last of the roof as darkness fell. It was amazing to see a cabin materialize from the natural resources of the mountain. In a way, it was still hard to believe this was our new home and that I was married now. It sometimes seemed as if I was looking at someone else's life unfolding before my eyes, but all it took was an embrace or a smile from Matthew to reassure me I was on the right path. I understood now how Ma had unflinchingly left the familiar world back East for the untested West. I somehow knew she had felt the same way for my father as I did for Matthew. I had always accepted my life without my father as simply one of life's paths refused to me, but now, as a married woman, I was grieved to think Ma had lost her one love so early. Matthew was right; she had to be a strong woman, that Irish mother of mine.

Although the men were exhausted after their hard day's work, when the violin and harmonica played, they were rejuvenated. Perhaps it was because it was so seldom that people had the opportunity for revelry. This was a rare time of celebration with so many friends and families gathered together. The children danced far beyond their bedtime until, at last, they dropped of weariness on the many blankets spread on the ground. The younger couples danced up a storm, despite the lack of a proper dance floor. Matthew and I even danced a couple of jigs ourselves under the full moon that graced our evening. The adults talked late into the night around the campfire, discussing family events and the latest mining discoveries. At last, we all turned in under the stars, the night cooling as it usually did in the mountains.

"It reminds me a little of what heaven will be like," Matthew whispered later as we settled down under our blankets. "Good will, peace, and joy among all of God's children. It would be heaven, indeed, if people could always help each other like this."

By midmorning of the following day, the last family had left, along with Ma and Amos. Where before I had appreciated nature's peacefulness, the quiet then seemed haunting. I knew entertaining that many people for long would have grown tiresome, but, for now, my mood rang of melancholy. I noticed Matthew was exceptionally quiet and figured he felt the same. It had been a splendid cabin raising.

Maggie's Way

Building their first home. Cabin raising with help from
neighbors. Drawn by Frenzeny and Tavernier.
Harper's Weekly, January 24, 1874

38

CATTLE CALL

The wonderful fragrance of fresh cut pine permeated our new home. With a shovel, I attacked the grasses and weeds that covered the earthen floor. Our first priority was framing the building; the plank floor could be worked on later. I pounded nails into the log walls near our bed to hang clothing and a few near the door for outer garments. Together, we raised the pipe from the potbelly stove through the opening in the roof.

With lumber purchased in Ouray, Matthew built shelves for food, a high bench to hold two tin basins (one for washing hands, one for dishes), and a dining table. Until chairs could be built, I had no problem using thick tree stumps cut to the appropriate height. The table, however, was beyond my expectations. I discovered one of Matthew's many skills was carpentry. He finished the table properly by sanding and oiling it with linseed oil until it took on a rich patina. As it turned out, Matthew had become a master of many trades to further the often-meager compensations of preaching.

It was a fair-sized cabin, compared to most of the small one-room structures built by new settlers. The largest cabin I had ever seen was built by a town council member with a flourishing mining supply business. It was a magnificent two-story building. Ours was modestly between the two extremes. We designated one side of the large open space for a kitchen and sitting area with the remaining space for sleeping quarters. Temporarily, we slept on a mound of hay and grasses covered with a large piece of canvas. My big project in the near future was to make a down-filled mattress before winter came. As I was more content to be outdoors, I gave little thought to the luxuries of furniture. Perhaps, during the long winter, I would feel differently, but that was a long way off. For now it was a dry place to sleep and a place of refuge from the frequent afternoon showers. It provided better shelter than the tent, which persistently leaked heavy drops on long rainy days.

Our four small windows needed shutters before winter, but for now, we hung canvas to keep out wind and rain. Two windows looked up at the wooded hills on the south side of the cabin with the others viewing the rolling hills and open valley below to the north. Matthew came up beside me as I gazed at the scenery. He wrapped his arms around me.

"What do you think, my Maggie girl?"

"Of the cabin?" I asked.

"Of the cabin, of marrying me, of everything."

"The cabin is wonderful," I said. "I guess you'll do too. Better than some of those rangy looking miners I've seen." I darted for the door in full anticipation of retaliation. The chase was on, with Matthew's longer legs soon overriding my pace. He grabbed me, and we fell to the ground in laughter. Though we had worked long, hard days ever since our wedding, we always managed to find some time in the day for fun and laughter.

"So are you ready for a trip, my lady?" he asked.

I propped my head on one elbow in rapt attention.

"It's time to go on a cattle drive."

The sun reached for the horizon; its rays stretching to surmount the rocky heights. We adjusted cinches and tightened ropes on packs. The sunrise wove violet ribbons through the clouds that hovered above the eastern peaks. The lone clouds raced through the sky and soon dispersed. It would be a fair day. We headed out, not bothering with breakfast. The morning dew glistened in the morning sunshine. Long, blue shadows from the trees fell in dramatic contrast to sunlit grasses. The birds chirped and twittered as we set off for our trip to Gunnison to buy cattle. The light gave off that fantastic effect that occurs during early morning, exclaiming God's magnificent handiwork. At these times, His glory was luminous.

My heart raced in anticipation of the long journey with Matthew. I realized then how much I had missed the packing trips through the mountains. We had kept busy on our new homestead, but I saw how much I had come to value outdoor excursions. Along with producing a decent livelihood, I was partial to ranching because there was always a ready excuse to check on the animals, herd them to summer pastures, gather them for branding or calving, or take them down to lower winter pastures. It was a job demanding time spent outdoors, which is exactly what I desired.

"You look as cheeky as if you had just robbed the biggest bank in Denver and gotten away with it," Matthew said, grinning at me.

"Happy to be out on the trail again," I answered. "It is a glorious day."

"It's a beauty for sure, just like my saucy bride."

Matthew often bestowed compliments, despite the fact that I continued to dress in my trousers and men's shirts. I knew he liked it when I was dressed up for church services, but it was not practical for the work we had been doing. By now I was uncomfortable wearing a dress, and my Matthew, true to his word, accepted me as I was.

Down Dallas Divide we rode, two riders and a pair of packed mules. Mo and Joe carried our bedrolls and food supplies for the trip. Compared to what they had packed for the mines, the loads must have ridden like feathers. I liked to think they enjoyed the outing as well.

It was late afternoon when Matthew spied a mule-deer buck heading down to a creek. He told me to wait while he went after it. I got down from my horse and stretched the tight muscles in my legs; we had ridden many miles without a break. Several minutes later, the report of his rifle sounded. I waited, occasionally scanning the thick brush that lined the stream. Finally, Matthew appeared with the animal strapped across the rump of his horse. My mouth watered as I anticipated the back-strap steaks we'd savor that night.

In Gunnison, we left behind most of our hard-earned savings in exchange for the yearling cattle. We would have found better prices on the Front Range, where raising cattle was fast becoming a growing business. The eastern prairie now teamed with large herds throughout the grasslands, with many of the animals coming from Texas. However, it was worth it to us to avoid further travel.

Our yearlings were crosses between Texan and graded shorthorns. Our funds being limited, we were able to buy only nine yearling cows and one promising bull. It would take several years to build up a herd. Matthew was not worried, confident that God would provide for us as long as we did our part. He reminded me of the biblical story of Jacob's flock of sheep proliferating despite Laban's sly tries at cheating Jacob at every turn.

Before we headed home, we had a bit of a holiday. Matthew had reserved a little money aside for shopping. He insisted I buy a new black wool hat; my freighting hat was a bit on the ragged side. We shopped for new warm shirts and new trousers for each of us. The storekeeper appeared a bit befuddled for a moment when I asked to try them on first. Since Matthew was there, though, he recovered his surprise and seized our money.

Last of all, Matthew insisted on a new dress. I protested, explaining I had two adequate garments back home. He insisted I must dress properly for dinner that evening, as he was taking me to the finest restaurant in town.

"Matthew, our money is almost gone."

"Listen, woman, a man gets married only once in his lifetime, and my mind is set on taking my new bride to dinner and, afterwards, a night on a feather mattress at a fine hotel."

I could see his mind was made up. On these rare occasions, I was learning it was best to back down. Usually it wasn't anything I couldn't live with. Matthew was not a hard man; he was kind and considerate.

I was glad afterward, for it was a memorable dinner. The hotel held its own with the finest establishments in Denver. We dined on duckling in wine sauce, glazed carrots, and twice-baked potatoes topped with cheddar. For dessert, we sampled a totally foreign concoction: cheesecake with canned strawberries.

Matthew claimed I was a beautiful, glowing bride, but I think my appearance was due more to my first glass of wine. It was a French wine called Chardonnay. Matthew was proud as a peacock to show me off. Since he never forced me into being a woman I was not, I let him savor the treat of having me dressed up, hair curling down, feminine as any girl had a right to be. Groomed with a haircut at the barbers, a bath in the hotel copper tub, and a fresh shave, he was a fine-looking man. The two of us caught many looks from our fellow diners. Nevertheless, I was happy that I didn't have to spend my life attired in the tightly-corseted dress.

The real work began on the long ride back. We rode fanned out in opposite directions behind the bull and nine yearlings. If a few aimed in the wrong direction, the rider on that side was responsible for guiding them back into the fold. At times, an energetic yearling ran off from the herd in protest. One of us would gallop off after the troublemaker, working our horse hard until the rebel was back in place.

The wind erupted in gusts as we rode along the winding Gunnison River. We followed it through the deep cliff breaks. Across from us, the monumental ridges stood at attention, throwing shadows far below. That first night, we ate a quick meal of coffee, beans, and side pork and waited for the tired cattle to lie down before we could rest. I don't remember sleeping so hard, yet at the first crack of dawn, I woke at the slightest rustling of a yearling like a mother attuned to her baby throughout the night. Our breakfast consisted of jerky washed down with water from the small canteens tied to our saddle horns.

A few days later we returned to our home site with relief, the vision of our cabin like a mirage, the sight still fresh to our eyes. We kept an eye

Maggie's Way

on the cattle grazing below until darkness came, and we settled in for an early evening.

The next day we began chinking clay-like mud in between the logs of the cabin. We labored with this for a full week. I knew it was imperative to prepare the cabin for winter, but still I became impatient and irritable. It was so much to do at once, and I was not accustomed to cooking meals everyday. My mood seemed to wear off on Matthew until we were soon avoiding each other.

After the work was completed on the cabin, Matthew declared a holiday was in order. He proposed a short excursion into the hills — just what I needed. We saddled up the next morning after a leisurely breakfast. Navigating the switchback angles of a game trail, we rode ever higher. The further we rode, the more heavily forested the hills became. Occasionally, the terrain opened up to crystal clear creeks flowing through small quiet meadows. At one point, we scared up three tawny mule deer that bounced away in their characteristic manner.

After two hours, we came upon a creek cascading over a rocky embankment. It plunged twenty feet below to a small pool surrounded by luminous white aspen. We agreed at once that this was our picnic spot. I had packed leftover fried blue grouse and corn muffins cooked in the Dutch oven the night before. Afterward, we dined on fresh raspberries picked on our ride up.

The rushing of the waterfall trembled behind us as a fine mist fell over us. We reclined on a blanket, halfway dozing in the sunshine, complacent with the thought of no pressing chores. It was a lazy day spent enjoying each other. Before we left for home, Matthew could not resist sifting through the gravel in the stream. Soon we were both absorbed in looking for color in the rocks. Alas, we didn't come up with even a single flake, but the day had not disappointed me.

"We didn't strike it rich today, Mrs. Harding. I guess I'll have to settle for a kiss."

As I closed my eyes, I remembered a kiss once before in a stream. My arms went around his neck, and I tried hard not to laugh as I recalled how I had once resisted the strange preacher man.

Maggie's Way

39

PLACERVILLE

It didn't take long until Matthew was ready to start up preaching again, so off to the new settlement of Placerville we went. On the way, we came upon an occasional prospector winding down from the hills, a few homesteading families, and one couple in a wagon en route to Placerville. It was not much of a town, as minerals had only recently been discovered. It had the look of an early settlement: tents, makeshift shacks, and a few log buildings in various stages of construction. Two hopeful merchants were set up for business under canvas tents, and one optimistic fellow displayed wares straight from his wagon.

We nailed small posters announcing Sunday's service on trees, fences, and wagons, as permitted by the owners. Matthew had the posters printed up years ago in Denver, leaving a blank spot for penciling in the date and time of services. A few prospectors scoffed at the posters, but several women were happy to see a bit of civilization could be had for their families. Matthew knew it would be a slow start, but he reminded me that the Gospel needed preaching to all the ends of the earth, including this one.

Four days later, we were back for Matthew's first service in the fledgling settlement. He picked a site under a big cottonwood near the creek. I helped clear the debris of fallen branches, and Matthew found some thick logs left over from cutting firewood to use for stools; otherwise, the grass would have to do.

I dressed up as I always did for service, one of the few times I forsook my regular attire. The midmorning sun warmed as we waited the twenty minutes before service. No early arrivals had appeared. I hoped for Matthew's sake that people would show . . . he would be so disappointed if no one came. I grew increasingly anxious, but, when I looked at Matthew, it was as if he had not a worry in the world. He looked perfectly at ease.

I looked over his shoulder as he checked his pocket watch; fifteen minutes remained before the service. Then I saw one middle-aged woman in the distance walking in the direction of the meeting tree. Matthew greeted her warmly when she arrived and offered her the single blanket we had spread over the grass.

How humiliating, I thought, to have one person show. Knowing my husband, he would preach if it turned out to be only a single soul. Ten minutes before service two young women, one with an infant in her arms, strolled up, smiling as if this was a regular occurrence. With gratefulness, I returned their smiles. Then an old weathered prospector arrived. An unlikely candidate, I thought. Knowing how superstitious miners could be, I wondered if he came to have a little of the Almighty's providence rub off on him, hoping this would be the lucky trick that finally caused him to strike it rich.

It was almost time for the service to begin as two men strode up to sit beside the women. Six people. Seven, if you counted the babe. I looked over at Matthew, who was nonplused; in fact, he seemed energized by all of this. Not me. This nervousness was wearying.

"I am happy to see all of you today. I'm Matthew Harding, and this is my wife, Maggie."

All heads turned my way, and I tried to give my best smile.

"I've been preaching over in Ouray, but Maggie and I were married earlier this summer and are now homesteading several miles east of here. I am looking forward to talking to all of you after the service, but now let us bow for a prayer to begin worship."

So the service began with the wee congregation, but, as the Bible says, "Where two or three are gathered . . ." Matthew asked for song requests and then led the singing. He had a good voice, strong enough to carry the small group even without an organ. His message was about Jesus's sermon on the mount. A fitting theme, I thought, for our first outdoor service. At the end, he passed a tin plate, asking only for what the Lord would lay on their hearts without causing any undue hardship.

Afterward, Matthew motioned me to his side, and we visited with each individual and family. Everyone thanked him for the good sermon and looked forward to more. Except for the commitment to one service in Ouray each month, he would hold services here every Sunday. I was suddenly awash in the knowledge of how my life was shifting. Me, a preacher's wife? I would never have predicted that.

The middle-aged woman, Mrs. Gustafson ("Roberta" was her given name), was the first to offer lunch, and I knew we were obligated. She served a simple fare of fried venison, biscuits, and coffee, but it was fine and one less meal I had to cook.

Maggie's Way

How the summer vanished. The first of September was upon us before we knew it. Matthew secured a job in Placerville, building shelves and counters for a new general store. It would take a few days for him to finish the work. He thought our cattle would be fine for two days, so we remained in Placerville while he worked.

At the end of the first day, I waited for Matthew's return to the camp where we had pitched our tent. I saw him at last in the distance, and, unable to wait, I dashed up to him.

"Don't you look like the mouse who caught the canary," Matthew said after greeting me with a kiss. We walked to our camp hand in hand as I began my entreaty.

"After spending all our savings, we're going to need a little extra money to see us through the winter. What do you think of me bringing in a little money too?"

"And how would that be, Maggie?"

"I was talking to Roberta today. Her husband is bringing in a load of stock for his store, and one of the mines needs supplies brought up tomorrow. He is overwhelmed with stocking his shelves, so I offered to go for him, since we're here anyway. Of course, I said I would have to ask you first."

Matthew studied me.

"I would return by evening."

"I can see you have your heart set on it," he said. "It looks like you're going to have a busy day tomorrow."

I gave him a big hug and dished up a plate of food for him from the Dutch oven simmering nearby. The rest of the evening, Matthew seemed rather subdued. I supposed he was weary from working all day: sawing and pounding and all that it took for his carpentry. As for me, I forced myself to relax and get some sleep for the long day ahead.

The next morning, we set off to work. I had Sierra in tow behind me at the end of the lead rope. Matthew walked with me to the Gustafson's store. Roberta's husband, Ben, awaited my arrival with the mules already packed and ready to go. Matthew paid heed as Gustafson gave me directions and a small hand-drawn map for my journey. While Gustafson adjusted a strap on one of the mules, Matthew asked if I understood the directions.

"You heard yourself how clearly he spelled it out, Matthew."

Ten minutes later, I kissed my husband goodbye and mounted my horse. Equipped with my slicker, I tucked my braids into my new wool felt hat. One thing that never changed was my revolver, which went everywhere with me. An exception was made when I dressed for Sunday services, at which time I packed it in my saddlebag. I looked back and waved once more to Matthew before he was out of sight.

It was exhilarating to pack mules into the mountains again. I enjoyed traveling with Matthew on our trip to Gunnison, but there was something special about a trip into the mountains by myself. It was easier to miss nuances when traveling with another person. Packing gave me time to ponder nature's beauty and wonder.

I knew Matthew had not been thrilled to see me take the job, even though we needed the money. We had a bare start on building a herd, and it was too late in the season to plant a garden. He went along with the idea because he saw how much I wanted to go. I had seen the effort he made to give me a smile goodbye, but I was not going to allow his response to ruin my trip. I had reason to savor this expedition, perhaps my last.

I had missed my woman's monthly visitation.

40

JOURNEY INTO DARKNESS

Although my appetite was fine, I avoided coffee first thing in the morning, as tea proved more soothing to my stomach. I had not said anything to Matthew because, along with not being sure, I was determined not to be treated like a delicate flower. Miscarriages could occur, but I had been around enough animals to know that either the seed would take root or there was not much one could do about it. Convinced that normal activities my body was accustomed to would have no adverse effect on the baby, I continued life as usual. Weeks before we were married, I had ruminated about the consequences marriage brought, namely pregnancy and child raising. At times it had frightened me, for it spelled great limitations to my life. I concluded that I was marrying a man who would not keep me cabin bound. He said himself that he knew the woman he was marrying, and he had proved that last evening. Knowing I could not live without Matthew, I had come to accept the restrictions babies would bring to my life. After acknowledging the reality of the situation, I explored as many remedies as I could find. Noting the way Indian women carried their babes showed me how to ride with an infant packed on my back. Toddlers from ranching families learned to ride at remarkable ages. I prayed that this child would be a boy, for fathers did not coddle their sons as they did their daughters.

Brilliant sunshine glittered over the turning quakies. I followed a creek for a distance and then found the path I had been directed to. I needed this day for myself, an adventure to reassure me that even a child would not change who I inherently was. I knew I would love our children, but, being young, I was apprehensive about all the changes.

Just then a large, dark animal scurried off into the woods, scared off by the bells on the mules' harnesses. It was the first black bear I had seen, and it was a thrill to catch sight of the brute. The Utes believed that bears were sacred and symbolized good luck to those who were fortunate to see one. Perhaps it was God's way of reassuring me all would be well.

By midday, I arrived and found the new silver mine in the initial stages of its development. A small mound of tailings was already forming on the hillside. The owner of the mine, Jake Talbott, was a cordial sort. I introduced myself. He had heard of Matthew and promised to go with his wife soon to one of the services. Then he surprised me with an unexpected offer. He asked if I wished to see the inside of the mine. Most miners were superstitious and believed it bad luck for a woman to go into a mine.

"The miners are off to town t'day," Jake said, "for a well-deserved day off. I don't have no qualms showing it to ya."

I had always speculated about what the mines looked like beneath the earth. I wanted to investigate at least one in my lifetime, and it seemed providential that the opportunity was arising now.

"I'll take you up on your offer, Jake."

He gave me a candlestick to fasten in the band of my hat, lighting it once I had my hat back on. Less careful of his own, he lit the candle first and tucked it onto his grimy hat. Into the damp, dusky tunnel we proceeded, walking a short distance before we started down a vertical passage. He went first to lead the way, and I followed him, stepping onto the crude wooden ladder that had been built to accommodate the shaft. Where the candles gave immediate illumination on the rock wall, I could see slight variations of the earth's colors. As we drifted through the dark abyss guided by only two candles, I did not envy the miners who worked the earth's bowel.

I began to reconsider the wisdom of this venture. Sporadically, dampness dripped onto my face or hands. After a seventy-five foot drop, we came out onto a short tunnel where we stooped to avoid hitting our heads on the rock-hewn ceiling. Then it opened to a stope, a great empty cavity left as ore was removed. It was lit up with torches, and Jake demonstrated how a miner worked with a pick, chipping into the rock walls. It caused a terrific noise that resounded in the hole. He pointed out the veins of silver in the walls and explained how they were formed in the same manner as gold: hot subterranean water circulated through the underground rock, depositing the silver in fractures that eventually formed veins. Jake suggested we head back to the surface if I was to return before nightfall. I concurred, as I had begun to feel nauseous with the weight of the heavy dark rocks closing in on me. Concentrating on my footage on the rungs going up kept the sickness at bay. Surely, he would not appreciate a sick woman in the close quarters of the mine.

At last breathing fresh air again, the blinding sunlight seared my eyes. Now that it was over, I did not regret exploring the inner workings of a mine, a mystery that had always lingered as I packed up and down the mountains. However, I didn't plan to see the innards of the earth again. The great outdoors would do just fine for me.

Maggie's Way

Tired but in good humor, I returned to my husband, who met me halfway from camp. Back at camp, Matthew cooked for me. After taking my fill, I sat back to relax by the campfire. The dear even made me tea. I related my adventure in the mine.

"It sounds like you had quite an exciting day." Matthew studied his mug of tea.

I walked over and knelt next to him, placing my hands in his.

"Matthew, you needn't worry. I won't be going on many adventures without you for a while."

He tried to appear nonchalant, but I could tell he was paying special attention to my words.

"It appears we will have an adventure of our own soon."

41

INSTINCT

As soon as the words escaped my mouth, I questioned the wisdom of telling him so soon.

"What adventure is that, Maggie?"

I could not take it back.

"I suspect a little Matthew is on his way."

"Already?"

He grinned at me before he scooped me up, swinging me round until I thought I would be sick this time.

I made him promise he would not treat me like an invalid, or, I warned him, I would head for the hills. I would not be told I could not ride or work. He grinned at my stubbornness, but he knew I was serious. We agreed not to announce the pregnancy for several months. I could tell that would be difficult for Matthew; he was bursting to tell someone.

Being in the motherly way, I became moody at times. Often I felt cranky, at other times weepy. It was one such evening when I was feeling the latter that I confessed my looming fears.

"Maggie," Matthew said. He softly stroked the hair at my temple. "We'll work on our ranch together, and we'll raise our family together too. You know I'm not going to delegate you to a sentence of domestic confinement."

He stopped to wipe at the tears falling down my face, something he rarely saw from me.

"I'm right by your side, girl, and I always will be."

I knew he was a man of his word, and it began with his helping with the cooking, as I was often tired in those first months. Luckily, he was a good cook. Once again, I thanked God to be so fortunate. To find a man like Matthew was far more rare than discovering gold in these hills.

We labored to finish our work before winter. One of the first things Matthew built was a privy out of special consideration for me. He finished the shutters for our windows on the cabin, and then we began stocking up firewood, anticipating what would be required for the winter. Matthew hauled the logs down, cutting them into stove and fireplace lengths. I piled them on a makeshift travois with one of the mules dragging it back to the cabin. We had to go a bit further out for wood, since I refused to strip the hillsides close to our cabin. Next, he built a small shed to keep our saddles, harnesses, and other leathers dry from the coming winter snows. My weariness had disappeared after those first couple of months, and, long-waisted that I was, I still did not show when dressed.

Tomorrow Ma and Amos were arriving for a visit. The weather would end those trips once the snow built up on the trails. That evening, Matthew and I set out to hunt for a deer; my desire was to serve fresh venison to our guests. We crept through the woods as the shadows lengthened, rarely talking, whispering if we did. We kept a careful watch until at last Matthew motioned me to stop. I peered through the trees until I caught sight of two large deer that had not spotted us. We were downwind from them, so they had not caught our scent. Matthew motioned me to shoot. I aimed and fired. The sound cracked through the hills, breaking the silence like a sudden thunderstorm as it reverberated into the distance. I saw one animal fall while the other dashed to safety.

We walked over to find the animal had not suffered; it had been a clean kill straight through the heart. Matthew proceeded with a variation of what Indians do upon killing an animal, which is to thank the animal's spirit for the gift of sustenance it gives through its death. Matthew thanked our Creator for the gracious gift He had given us that day. He then gutted the animal while I went back for Mo to help pack it out of the woods. Living on the land, we killed only what we needed and never just for sport. Nevertheless, this was a far more humane way for a wild animal to die than starving during a hard winter.

The next morning, I kept an eye out for the buckboard, which would announce Ma's arrival. I marinated four back-strap steaks in a special seasoned sauce I had created, a favorite of Matthew's. The doe would be exceptionally tender in contrast to a buck in mating rut.

Our company arrived as I finished kneading dough for biscuits. I wiped my hands on a cloth and hurried out to meet them. Embraces and greetings done, Amos sauntered over the rise to talk to Matthew, who was cutting wood. I helped Ma carry four pies (plenty for their visit and a couple to leave with us), a twenty-pound bag of potatoes, a sack of earth-covered carrots, and a package of side pork from the butchers. Rely on Ma to feed us.

I poured two cups of tea, and we found a sunny place to sit outdoors. The quakies were beginning to lose their leaves, the gold glittering across the ground. Ma began to tell me of all the local news, but none was as vivid as the news about Lily.

"She's run off with her young man," Ma announced.

"Before they even married?" I quipped. Then I realized what a silly thing to say, considering her former occupation. "They left town, then?"

"That they have, and with my day's profit."

"I knew that girl couldn't be trusted!"

"If that's the worst that's ever done to me," Ma said, "I am not the worse for wear."

"After everything you've done for her." I was indignant.

"She left a note that she would repay me some day."

"That I have to see."

"The Lord told us to give our cloak to others; He never said only if they repay us in return."

I could see I would have to drop my indignation, for even Matthew would agree with her.

The next day Ma and I went for a lovely walk together. I told her all about our services in Placerville and the people we were meeting. That evening, after the chill coaxed us inside, Matthew stoked up the open stone fireplace. The men took turns telling us stories, which either drew convulsive laughter or wide-eyed wonder. I suspect most of the tales were embellished for their entertainment value. They certainly were engaging, and we all enjoyed the evening.

As they prepared to set off for Ouray on the third day, Ma sat aboard the wagon as Amos and Matthew visited near the rear of the buckboard. She asked if I had been feeling well.

"Fine, Ma. Why do you ask?"

"I always felt good, too, when I was carrying you."

42

LONG COLD WINTER

"Well, Margaret," Amos broke in. "Are we ready?"

"That we are," she answered.

Matthew came around to kiss Ma on the cheek. I saw her whisper something to him.

I stood dumbfounded as they rode away.

"So, you couldn't refrain from telling the soon-to-be grandmother," Matthew said.

"I never said a thing."

He looked puzzled.

"But she told me to watch over our new mother, just now as I said goodbye to her."

It was early-on in the pregnancy; I was certain I did not show.

"I don't know how that woman does it, but somehow she knew."

Matthew and I laughed. He asked if I thought the news would be all over Ouray by morning.

"Oh, no. She'll keep it to herself, but, you can be assured the next time we see her, she'll have several baby blankets quilted, not to mention sundry articles of baby clothing."

"I'm sure," he agreed, "if she sews anything like she cooks."

Ma had left large flour sacks filled with feathers and bundles of fabric remnants bought at Amos's store. As the cold weather approached, my new project became making quilts and a down mattress. Looking back, it was a godsend for one who could easily go stir crazy during the confinements of winter. I finished the mattress first, longing for a more comfortable bed as my pregnancy progressed. Before winter was spent, I completed a quilt for our bed, one tiny quilt for the babe, and two quilt tops to be finished another winter. Matthew joked that I had found my calling at last, at which I hurled a pillow at him.

In January, we were snowbound for two days after a blizzard abruptly enveloped us. Matthew ventured out to bring in needed firewood, which was stockpiled next to the cabin, and to clear snow from the door and windows. I melted buckets of snow for our water needs. The wind was fierce, howling for forty-eight hours nonstop. Matthew read aloud the story of Jonah trapped in the mouth of the whale, and I thought I understood how the prophet must have felt, cooped up in that strange place. Though we kept the fires going full blast, it was so cold we had to wear our outer coats. Matthew slept fitfully at night, afraid to sleep deeply and risk the fires dying out. He feared his bride and mother-to-be would freeze to death without his diligence. In the morning, we woke to small drifts of snow inside our cabin, formed from wind-blown snow seeping through cracks around the windows and door. We stayed in bed as late as we dared.

When the storm ceased on the third morning, we were fearful of what condition the animals would be found in. Matthew made me stay inside while he rode off to check. I fumed at not being allowed to go, but he didn't know how far they had wandered in search of shelter. He had that look that told me it would do no good to protest. He had kept his promise of not treating me as a helpless invalid, but he had his limits. And the aftermath of this terrific storm was one of them. Later, he admitted he had feared I would get upset if I had seen several dead animals.

While he was out, I tried to piece my quilt and work out the anger of being left behind, when a thunderous roar and shaking sounded overhead. After the stillness returned, I tentatively opened the door, only to find it would not budge but a few inches. I peered out with my face pressed against the door and realized what had happened. The snow had accumulated on top of the roof and had melted with the clearing sky and sunshine, convulsing to the ground in one big collapse. I had to wait patiently for Matthew's return. Two hours later, my imprisonment within the cabin ended.

It turned out we did not lose any cattle, but they had indeed been stressed and required careful watching for the next few days. Matthew reported he had cleared icicles from the nostrils of the animals, including our poor horses and mules. Luckily, it was the last storm of the season with that degree of sustained wind and snow.

Spring came at last. We alternated services in Placerville between two of the parishioner's cabins. Matthew and I were getting to know the people of Placerville; it was becoming our community. During the winter, we ventured to Ouray only during fair weather. My lengthening pregnancy lessened our travels, although I was feeling well.

By March, my belly rounded out to a soft, warm mound. For months my trousers had not been buttoned in the fly: instead, they were held together by an additional piece of cloth to which I had added buttons. I was now wearing Matthew's shirts, which were large enough to cover my

Maggie's Way

belly. One single Sunday-go-to-meeting dress gathered below the bust, accommodating my ample belly during my remaining pregnancy.

One day, Matthew and I rode out to check cattle. As we saddled up, he looked over at me. He studied me as I placed one foot in the stirrup and pulled myself up into the saddle.

"Are you uncomfortable, Maggie?" he asked.

"Feeling fit as a fiddle," I quipped.

"Do you feel it's wise?" Matthew's eyes looked into the distance, avoiding my eyes.

"Am I an invalid now?" My mouth set hard as my hand clenched the saddle horn.

"No, that's not . . .what I intended . . ."

I took a deep breath. I compelled my self to be tolerant — though I didn't feel like it much. I reassured him that I had a strong, healthy body, convincing him that common sense riding would in no way harm our baby. I had had enough of winter's seclusion, and I insisted on accompanying him.

Checking on our new calves one spring day in April — about three miles west from our place — we discovered we had new neighbors. We came upon a man cutting wood for a cabin. A woman and young girl were cooking at an open fire nearby as we approached to introduce ourselves. Upon closer inspection, I saw they were native women. The same beautiful coal black hair adorned the younger girl, although her skin was lighter. She looked to be about the age of twelve.

The short, stocky man with a long beard introduced himself as Edward Tulling, a trapper and prospector. He explained he was a Frenchman whose English father had moved to France and soon after married his mother. As a young man, he had immigrated to America, ever moving further west.

They were living in a canvas tent during the frigid spring nights, but they wore heavy clothing and were apparently getting by. Edward insisted we stay for a cup of tea and corn cakes. He did not introduce us to his wife until after the tea was served. Edward spoke in rapid Ute; our names the only things I could make out. "My woman's name is Raven Eyes," he said, nodding toward his wife. Her eyes darted up and met mine. I nodded. The young girl kept to herself back by the tent, but I had the feeling she was watching for all her worth. Raven Eyes stayed behind us, sitting on a rock. Her broad face had the look common to the Ute tribe, and her braided hair was a glistening black, as were all full bloods. I was very careful not to stare, but occasionally I stole sideway glances at her. Each time, I found her eyes focused on the ground, but once I caught her eyes darting back from looking at me too. I smiled.

Edward looked to be in his mid-forties, his well-tanned face evidence of a life spent outdoors. Raven Eyes's face was without lines but had the look of a mature woman. I knew Indian women were competent horse-women and were well acquainted with the ways of the natural world. I suspected I would enjoy knowing this woman if we could communicate. I felt odd sitting there by the men as they talked about wildlife and mining while Edward's wife sat ignored in the background. Not knowing how she would react, I moved closer to her without making eye contact and sat on a nearby rock. I drank my tea without attempting to speak. At last, she turned to me and gestured with her arms as if she held an infant and then pointed to my midriff. I smiled and nodded my head. She smiled in return. She rose to pour more tea for the men and then returned to fill my cup. After a while, the young girl sidled up and sat down. She often looked my way when she thought I was not watching. Raven Eyes began speaking in Ute to the girl. How surprising it was when I heard an English name in the midst of the indecipherable sounds! Emily, it became clear, was the girl's name.

At last, we thanked our host and his wife and mounted our horses. Matthew encouraged Edward to bring his family to our cabin in the near future. As we began to move off, I turned around in my saddle as I heard Raven Eyes speak a halting "good . . . bye" followed by Ute dialect. Edward laughed and told us she had said, "Goodbye white woman in trousers." We laughed. I raised my hand in farewell.

"It appears you have a new friend," Matthew said.

"How I wished she spoke English," I said. I looked back once more and saw Edward tousle the top of the girl's head. Raven Eyes watched us still and raised an arm as I had earlier. Laughing, I waved goodbye once more.

I was constantly reminded of my condition whenever I bent forward, the baby pressing hard against my breastbone. By late May, I elected not to ride anymore; not because I couldn't still mount my horse, but because sitting was uncomfortable. Even in my final month, I wasn't as large as some women become, yet Matthew teased me about my large tummy. I intended on staying active this summer, even if it took strapping my baby on my back like a native papoose.

A week later, Matthew and I enjoyed a noon meal outside in the warm, balmy air that promised summer. The aspen and cottonwoods were begin-ning to bud out, and the first flowers were in bloom among the greening grasses. My tea that morning gave me some indigestion. I was also feeling the slight contractions that my body had practiced for months — temporary tightenings of the abdomen, lasting a few moments. A midwife in town had explained to me that it was nature's way to prepare for the final event. Perhaps the indigestion caused some discomfort for the baby, for when I was up and walking about it ceased. By early afternoon, I suggested we visit the Tullings. Matthew looked at me with a curious eye but indulged me as a woman in the late throes of a body growing with child.

Over his protest, I insisted I wanted to walk the three miles there, arguing it was good for both the baby and me. Matthew insisted we lead one of the horses in case the weather changed and we needed to hurry home. The fresh air and exercise were invigorating, and I felt no more tightness in my abdomen. It turned out to be indigestion after all.

The Tullings were surprised to see us, but they welcomed us with tea, fresh bread, and jam. Raven Eyes looked me over and made a motion with her hands that I assumed meant I was getting big. I smiled back. Halfway through my tea, I set the enamel tin cup down and could no longer sit with the pressure on my ribs. I motioned in what I hoped communicated the discomfort of sitting. My abdomen felt tight, and I experienced more slight contractions. Was my digestion no longer able to handle tea either?

I asked Edward to interpret for me, inviting his wife to go for a walk with me. She stood and nodded. We walked along the stream below their now-completed cabin. Immediately, I felt better. It is amazing what a good walk can do for the body. It was strange how at ease I felt with Raven Eyes, a person I couldn't even speak to. I sensed she was a woman with strength and inherent kindness in her spirit. Half an hour later, we returned to find the men in a discussion over the price of cattle and furs. When it became late afternoon, I suggested to Matthew we should be getting back. We both stood up to leave when Raven Eyes spoke to Edward. She chattered rapidly, raising her arms in emphasis, her eyes darting between her husband and Matthew and me.

Edward interpreted. "She says you must stay so she can help deliver your first baby."

43

MOTHERHOOD

I laughed. "That could be a few weeks; I don't think we want to wait that long," I answered.

There was more Ute chatter.

"She insists you are in labor now. You must not have your first alone, she says."

Matthew looked concerned and asked if I felt okay.

"Just the slight contractions I usually have throughout the day, Matthew."

Then I had the strongest contraction up to that time. Unconsciously, my hand reached for my abdomen, an action not lost on my three observers.

"It won't hurt to stay the night if Edward is willing. I don't want to deliver the baby myself if there is an experienced woman around."

I protested briefly, but saw Matthew was going to insist. I acquiesced to the majority opinion.

Two hours went by, and the pain would lessen whenever I walked around. Raven Eyes finally insisted I stop walking. I think she knew I was delaying the process and decided it was time to let the baby come. I was not so sure about all of this, now that the time had arrived. To be honest, I would not have minded delaying this part a month or two. It was like being caught in an avalanche: once you were in it, it was too late to do anything but let nature take its course. Raven Eyes sensed my apprehension and talked soothingly in Ute as she escorted me into the cabin. She motioned for me to lie down on a soft palette and began wiping my face with a moist cloth every few minutes.

The light labor pains lasted two hours and the intense final stage a remarkable hour and a half. Later, I was told that it was common for the first baby to take eight to twelve hours. When the time between contractions shortened, Raven Eyes shooed Matthew away. Only the young girl was allowed to remain, and she began gathering things for her mother. Raven Eyes made me drink a slightly bitter tea, the like of which I had never tasted. Herbs, I guessed. I had always heard that Indians were experts in choosing plants for various remedies. This one was either to lessen the pain or to quicken the birth. It was beyond my caring, for all I knew was the incredible pain. At last the baby arrived, crying balefully.

Raven Eyes cut the umbilical cord, wiped the infant, and presented him into my arms. My prayers were answered — I had my boy. Joshua Matthew Harding was the sweetest little thing I had ever laid eyes on. I examined his eyelids, which remained closed below the downy brown hair; his tiny nose and cherub lips, and the fragile little fingers, were fascinating. A few minutes later, Matthew entered. The furrowed brows changed to a face with a beaming smile of pride as he held his firstborn son. You would have thought we had invented the first baby, we were so beside ourselves. The next morning we headed home to begin our new life together as a family. I communicated through Edward my gratefulness to his wife, who looked content with the satisfaction of a job well done. She sent a large package of herbs home with me. Edward explained I was to have a cup of herb tea each day to prevent hemorrhaging and promote a speedy recovery. I bid farewell to my capable "doctor," to whom I made a private vow to teach the English language, as I knew we were going to be good neighbors. Edward promised to send a message to Ma via the mail carrier in Placerville, announcing her first grandchild was awaiting her arrival.

That night was the first of many long evenings to come. The baby awoke every two to three hours for feeding. We discovered the joy of parenthood came at the price of lost sleep. In the morning, Matthew made breakfast, the dear. Then he left to check on the cattle. As the baby slept, I started a kettle of soup and made a batch of bread dough. These tasks completed, my lack of sleep caught up with me. I climbed into bed, pulling up the down quilt, and had just nodded off when Joshua began to cry. I nursed him and snuggled him into bed with me. He started up again, so I checked his bottom. Dry and clean. I tried rocking him, to no avail. Tried jiggling him in my arms as I paced back and forth. The crying was non-stop. What more could I do? What was wrong with the baby, or what was I doing wrong? I placed him in the cradle and sat down on the opposite side of the room. I joined him in his wailing.

Perhaps my earlier leanings away from marriage had been prudent: maybe I wasn't meant to be a mother. How was I going to do everything right for a tiny, helpless babe who was totally dependent on me? And what did Matthew know? . . . as little as I. I cried until my eyes were swollen and my temples ached. At last the baby had cried himself to sleep. I nodded off as I sat in the chair. Then the door creaked open, and

Matthew stomped his boots at the door. He smiled over at me. My head jerked up. The baby began crying. I glared at him. At that, he turned and went back outdoors.

I waited for Ma's appearance, which I knew would come within a short time following the delivered message. I needed her experience and advice as soon as possible.

On the fourth day, my mother arrived, delighted to be a grandmother. She appeared with more baby paraphernalia and with most-welcomed advice for taking care of an infant. Matthew and I relaxed upon her arrival. With her calm exterior and patience, we soon felt there was hope for our incompetence.

After I nursed the baby, Ma took him from me and changed his diaper. She held the now-sleeping Joshua in her arms, her face aglow. It came to me then for the first time that surely she had anticipated more children for herself. Instead, she had been given a short-lived marriage to the man she loved and only one child, yet I had never heard her complain.

"Your life will change now, Maggie, but for the better, rest assured. You're blessed with a good man who is far more helpful than most husbands. You have a life that suits you and a man who caters to your stubborn Irish ways. You'll look back in later years, my dear one, and know how exceptional was your good fortune."

She lowered Joshua into the wooden rocking cradle Matthew had built for him. Ma walked over and kissed the top of my head before she turned to fix the midday meal.

"Ma, move closer to us," I blurted out. "Placerville could use a good restaurant."

She paused as she considered my request. "I'm quite settled in now, dear, but I'll think about it."

Frankly, I was surprised she would consider a move, but having a grandchild must weigh heavily in her decision.

"It'd be wonderful to have you closer, Ma."

She smiled as she continued her preparations.

My transition into motherhood went smoother as time went on. Within a few weeks, Raven Eyes showed me how to wrap up a "papoose" on my back, enabling me to join Matthew on horseback to check cattle each day. Never once did Matthew insist I stay home. He knew how important

Maggie's Way

it was that I get out, especially now with a new infant who required constant care.

That summer Matthew received several orders for furniture, which brought much-needed income. By word of mouth orders arrived weekly, many from Ouray. It worked out well for us with the new baby, as Matthew could do the work back at our homestead. Once he had several pieces finished, we loaded the wagon and took them to town. By the end of the summer, our savings enabled us to buy more cattle.

I was despondent the week Matthew left with Charlie Putnam, a man from our Sunday service, to bring back new cattle. Because I was nursing, there was no question of leaving Joshua with Ma. Regardless, I would never have risked those tender baby lungs to the dust and weather such a trip brought. I found myself taking on extra tasks to keep my mind off my exclusion from the trip. I mounted my horse with Joshua in tow and checked on the cattle. Each afternoon, we went for a quiet walk into the woods. Despite the daily tasks of cooking, cleaning, and infant care, the days without Matthew seemed long and cumbersome. I found myself yearning for the freedom I had before the baby came. I felt tremendously guilty for these thoughts, but there was no stopping them. They stormed into my mind uncontrollably, like a herd of cattle stampeding in a thunderstorm.

At last, Matthew returned. We now had thirty cattle, including the new calves born out of our original stock. We enlisted Edward's help to brand our new cattle, in return for two fresh sides of beef when winter came around. With the baby to care for, I couldn't be much help with the actual roping or branding, but I kept the fires stoked with wood for the irons. I cooked up a volume of bread, pies, and a big pot of stew for the busy men. Our brand was the double M, representing Matthew and Maggie.

"You'll need to make your husband a passel of sons, Maggie," Edward said. "You'll need the help as your herd increases."

I nodded my head and held my tongue. I had full intentions that my strong and capable daughters would work alongside us.

Although it was a rough start, my confidence as a mother grew. My metamorphosis from an independent young woman to a wife and mother was a transformation that surprised me most of all. Me, Maggie O'Malley, who almost panicked to the point of calling off my engagement to Matthew. The young, unconventional woman people sneered at, the trouser-wearing traitor to womanhood, was now a wife and mother. Yet, here I was still wearing trousers and riding side by side with my husband through the foothills of the mountains. Ma was so astute: without the right husband, I don't believe I could have done marriage and motherhood justice. I was truly fortunate and blessed.

And little Joshua Matthew Harding? Only the most beautiful child God ever created . . . dark, near-black hair and the cutest chubby cheeks made for kissing. His alert blue eyes looked out at us patiently, as if he knew we were doing the best we could. As time went on, he seldom cried, and then only to inform us of pressing needs. My instinct told me Joshua would be like his father: even tempered, easily seeing the joy and humor of life. Everything this child did was a miracle and a wonder to us, as I suppose it is for all parents of their firstborn. That summer went by quickly with so much to do. Our new family of three was a joyful one, for we now had one more person to love.

Maggie's Way

GOLDEN DREAMS

By the following summer, our herd had grown to eighty head. Joshua tottered around well, everything now within his inquisitive reach. He was as much at home on horseback as any cowboy as he rode in front of Matthew in the saddle. The little guy knew he was to behave while riding, but it did not require much coaching on our part; he took to it naturally. He loved going with us, moving the cattle, seeing all the sights. Only when he fell limp in the saddle sound asleep did I have to dismount and take a break while he napped.

Gratefully, I had not soon become with child again. Ma claimed nursing was a deterrent to pregnancy. She had decided to remain in Ouray, where she was quite woven into the fabric of the community. Her renown now preceded her; her food was recommended for miles around. "Be sure to stop at O'Malley's when you get there" was a common bit of advice given. A responsible young woman, Abigail Higgins, now worked for her, and Ma felt confident leaving her in charge of running the restaurant. So every month, save through the hardest part of the winter, she came visiting for four days at a time, driving a buckboard by herself. I insisted on giving her shooting lessons to accompany the rifle we gave her for self-protection, and she became quite a sharpshooter. Just as I had learned easily, she picked it right up. It must have been our Irish determination.

In September of 1879, news arrived of a massacre at Meeker in northern Colorado. Initially, we heard the savages had murdered an Indian agent named Nathan Meeker, destroyed his headquarters, and marched on the warpath. Throughout the state, people were stirred up when they heard Meeker's wife and adolescent daughter, along with another woman and her two children, had been taken as hostages. Ouray citizens were no exception; they became agitated as they read the newspaper accounts reporting the horror of white women held captive by savages.

We had privilege to another insight, however, through our neighbor Edward Tulling. By word of mouth through fellow fur trappers and Indian friends, he heard about Meeker's aim to mold the native hunters into farmers, treating them like children rather than the proud people they were. Meeker even withheld needed supplies as punishment for any resistance to his rigid methods and ideas. It is a grave danger when people see others as so foreign from themselves that they no longer view them as fellow human beings. I had seen this happen often with the way people viewed the Irish, the Mexicans, and the Negroes, but the Indians were the worst in many people's minds. Savages . . . the word itself conjured up visions of wild wolves gone mad.

By the following summer, my hope of teaching Raven Eyes the English language had been fulfilled. We communicated, albeit in a halting, abbreviated form of the language. Raven Eyes identified a common plant found in the mountains that she claimed would lengthen the time between pregnancies. I would have to gather and dry enough of it through the summer to last over the winter months. Joshua was a strapping two-year-old who now ate regular food ravenously. I was willing to try it, as my nursing had dwindled to one feeding in the morning and one before bedtime.

By 1880, the United States Census reported a population of 864 people residing in the town of Ouray proper, which had become a center of economic activity in the San Juans. Word reached us that the Virginius Mine had been sold for one hundred thousand dollars. The promises of exceptionally rich ore at the elevated site materialized into a very successful venture. In August, the peace-loving Chief Ouray died. White men had seized and devoured not only the valuable minerals, but also the proud Ute people whose land those riches had come from.

Placerville had not grown as feverishly as predicted. As a result, Matthew's services grew only slightly in attendance. Between raising cattle and his furniture work, Matthew preferred the small congregation.

Had Matthew and I lost our interest in placer mining? Heavens, no! That summer, we often took a break for a picnic and a day of gold panning. We found a promising stream two miles east of our place. Joshua joined in our gleeful celebration of discovering pan after pan of golden flakes. To his young mind, dancing in a stream and splashing water at each other were valid activities in themselves. The tiny glittering grains at the bottom of the pan were insignificant.

Matthew felt the site was lucrative enough to invest in a cradle, a rocking box with a sieve to filter the sand at one end while riffles on the other end caught gold as the sand and dirt washed over it. We brought our new contraption back from our last visit to Ouray but kept our discovery from all, even our neighbors. The discovery of gold could spread like a fatal fever, and, at this point, we did not actually know what we were dealing with.

After the third day of using the cradle, we realized we were in a good way. I had never seen so many flakes collected; they were filling a can just as one might have filled it with sand. This was on top of finding one odd-shaped nugget of fair size.

"Maggie, can you believe our good fortune?" Matthew gave me a generous hug.

"Papa, papa!" Our little lad stood with his arms held out, wanting his turn in dad's arms.

Matthew picked Joshua up and held him high above his head. He giggled as he was swung round and round.

That evening after Joshua was fast asleep, we took our evening tea around the campfire and discussed our next step.

"I'm anxious to know the value of what we have already collected," I said.

Matthew placed a gentle hand on mine.

"I believe we should hold off on that, Maggie."

My enthusiasm dampened.

"I think we should look for the mother lode instead." His eyebrow raised as the familiar grin appeared.

My heart beat faster as I pondered what tomorrow might bring.

After breakfast the next morning, we saddled up and left for our exploration. We rode past the stream where we had placer mined for over a week, then headed upstream in high hopes. Riding further, we scrutinized the landscape, at times stopping to investigate an outcropping or rock ledge where Matthew used a pick to crack away at the rock.

By mid-afternoon we were about to turn back, when my eye fastened on a boulder shimmering in the sunshine. I rode into the stream within a stone's throw of it. Dismounting my horse, I examined the stripe of glittering color, as water soaked into my boots. I yelled at Matthew to come. As he rode up quickly, his horse's legs splashed water over me. He dismounted, planting Joshua on the creek bank, and knelt down for a closer look. At last, he stood and turned to me with a solemn face. My hopes were dashed, and I felt quite silly to have thought a vein of gold might reveal itself in the open.

"It's just a rock with a stripe, Maggie," he began, "granite with stripes of quartz and ... gold."

It took a moment for my mind to override the lack of inflection in his voice. My head raised up then to focus on my husband's face. His gaze froze upon the stone. Then his voice rose in a shout of jubilation spreading into the small canyon like sudden thunder. Joshua's eyes widened at the voice he had never heard his mild-mannered father use. Then he tried his own toddler attempt at a shout of his own. For two hours, Matthew heaved the pick to pry the ore from the vein on the boulder. We rode home tired but elated, with a small canvas bag of gold to show for our effort.

The next morning, we returned to explore the immediate area surrounding the site. I kept Joshua out of harm's way while we watched Matthew work. He swung a pick at a rock overhang a hundred feet above the creek where the boulder stood. About the time I was going to suggest a break for lunch, Matthew let out a whoop, and I knew he had found it. I picked up Joshua, who was annoyed to be snatched away from his play with colorful rocks in the stream. Matthew took my face in his hands and kissed me hard.

"Look, woman!"

Joshua placed his little hands on my cheeks in imitation of his father and kissed me as I laughed.

"Joshua, look at the pretty rock." Where the pick had exposed the underlying ore, the horizontal vein of gold ran sweetly discovered.

"We are true miners after all, my love," I said to my husband.

Matthew picked up his small son in one arm and took my hand with his other. There in the August sun we danced an Irish jig to the accompaniment of Matthew's refrain of an invented song. It brought to mind a most bittersweet thought that Thomas O'Malley's dream of finding gold had come true after all. I looked at Joshua's sweet face and hoped God had allowed my father to look down at this moment in time. A hawk screamed suddenly, and I looked up to watch it fly high overhead. It circled above us for several minutes before it was lost on the horizon.

45

CATASTROPHES AND CHANGES

Keeping our discovery to ourselves, we hastened to Ouray to stake our claim. While I visited Ma, Matthew made inquiries on how to solicit investors from back East. Within the month, we were quietly showing the site to a representative of an investment firm in New York. He was an odd little English fellow clad in a derby hat. A mineralogist and a mining manager accompanied him during the inspection of the claim.

Five days later, we signed over our claim to eastern investors to the tune of five thousand dollars. Now we could build a proper frame house and add several head of cattle to our herd. Our mine (actually the investors' now) was worked over the next five years for a meager profit. As mines went, it never became a Virginius or a Mineral Farm success. But for the Harding family, the business transaction was the ticket to a successful cattle ranch.

In 1883, I turned the ripe age of twenty-five. The Harding family had grown to include two sons; Thomas Harding arrived three years after his brother, Joshua. Our two-and five-year-olds brought us much joy and laughter as our cattle business became well established. It was lucrative; after all, miners always needed feeding. At branding time, we hired local friends for this growing chore and paid them with a side of beef.

The winter of 1883 brought disaster to the Ouray mining district. After a storm dumped snow for three days and nights, snowslides exploded around the high amphitheater of the Virginius Mine. The miners thought the area safe from slides as the buildings stood high above timberline, but they were fatally wrong. With a tremendous amount of snow falling in a short time, a slide crashed into the boarding house. Four miners were killed, while two remained buried for over twenty-four hours before digging themselves out.

A party of men transported the bodies down from the mine the next day but not before disaster struck again. Deep snow lingered, draping the steep slopes, and another avalanche struck the rescue party. Thirty-two men were swept down the canyon, some a hundred feet, others as much as a thousand feet over a steep cliff. Out of the deadly silence that ensued, the miners began digging themselves out of the snow. Amazingly, all thirty-two men survived! However, the sled containing the bodies from the previous day's disaster remained buried until it was thought safe to search for it. Weeks later, when the bodies were brought down to Ouray, the photograph of the rescue party and sled of bodies was published in The Solid Muldoon newspaper. Life in the San Juans was laden with perils, none so great as for those men mining the monumental peaks.

The times were changing. With the year 1886, the town of Ouray watched the construction of a grand hotel. I will never forget the first day I saw the finished structure. The Beaumont was built with a French influence to its architecture. Its multiple facades gave it a definite European flavor to the tune of eighty-five thousand dollars. A large tower-like peak rose high above the street, as the building reached out perpendicularly on each side with three stories. Matthew described to me the grand open staircase, which ascended from the main lobby. Women did not use the front entrance, as it accessed the bar and billiards rooms and was thus considered inappropriate for use by a lady. I thought this ridiculous, considering we were a far cry from the society of Boston or New York.

By 1887, I was the proud mother of four boys. I laughed as I saw how others must see me in town: four little ones in tow like a mother duck with her brood. Joshua was nine years, Thomas six years; there was one-year-old Henry and fifteen-week-old James. I found the herbs to be effective, but the summer's dryness had not produced an abundant crop. Busy with three children, I didn't persevere in searching for the herb. I would be more conscientious in the future, as it was difficult to have two babies. Matthew, bless his soul, helped me even more during these years. My loving husband was indeed a treasure. I anticipated Ma's visits for the extra help she brought each month. Joshua and Thomas were old enough to be great helpers now, too.

The first train arrived in Ouray in 1887 — the Denver & Rio Grande Railroad. Otto Mears, the Russian immigrant, had finished a toll road over Red Mountain three years earlier, which many said could not be done. It was touted near and far as the greatest achievement in road building, as it was built through the uppermost crown of the steep and treacherous Red Mountains. His toll road conveyed the profits of the Red Mountain Mining District to Ouray, where previously Silverton had been the more accessible mining town. Though the road proved an advantage for mining and commerce, I was told that it was so narrow in most places that two wagons could not pass without one backing up.

Maggie's Way

My darling husband surprised me on our tenth anniversary with a sumptuous dinner in the Beaumont Hotel's dining room. After ten years of marriage, Matthew still proved to be a romantic, but it was in the many sweet things he did for me daily that proved his love.

46

NEARING THE CLOSE OF A CENTURY

The San Juan Stage Lines now transported passengers and the U.S. mail to Placerville and then onto Telluride. When a saloon keeper from Telluride saw Matthew's work at the general store in Placerville, he promptly placed an order for a dozen-and-a-half bar stools. After completion of three or four stools, Matthew sent them by way of the stagecoach, the driver securing them with ropes to the top.

In 1890, I delivered another child, and, much to the surprise of all, it was a girl. I named her Anne, my mother's middle name, but we called her Annie. I figured we had enough Margarets already in the family. I was set on raising a strong, independent daughter in our predominately male family. I knew I had my work cut out for me, convincing her brothers to let her grow into a capable woman.

A year later, Matthew wanted me to wean Annie early because he had a trip planned for the two of us — where, he would not say. On our anniversary, Ma watched our crew while we went on the Circle Route Stage, traveling over Red Mountain Pass on Otto Mears's famous road. It was a breathtaking ride, albeit bumpy and rough in the coach, as we rode the dirt road with steep cliffs plummeting off one side. We saw the oft-talked-about town of Silverton at last, and there I boarded my first train as an adult.

Travel by train was luxurious compared to the jarring stagecoach, and I found it easier to appreciate nature's beauty. We followed evergreen-lined streams and then climbed high above them, at times looking down a steep cliff where the rails hovered on the edge.

Later in our journey, I found myself once again in the town of Denver. I was amazed at the tremendous growth since the day Ma and I left for new horizons. While in Denver, we ordered more cattle. Our flourishing business could now afford to pay a drover to drive them to Ridgway.

Time scurries when you are raising children, making a living, and just plain living life. In 1892, I gave birth to another baby. It would be our last child — another girl — as the following year Matthew came down with the mumps. For a few weeks I feared I would lose my husband, as he nearly died from contracting the disease so late in life. It would have been

Maggie's Way

unfortunate if he had caught it early in our marriage, preventing us from having children. Our six children blessed our lives immensely, and I loved them far more than I had ever thought possible.

Our last child was Margaret. Yes, I relented and put a third Margaret in our family, as I could not resist giving the legacy of my mother to both my girls. Over the years, I told the stories of everything their grandmother had experienced and accomplished. I suspect the Lord has quite a sense of humor. He knew with baby girls in the family I would be ever on guard, ensuring they were not coddled.

The following year, 1893, was notable as Colorado gave the right to vote to its female citizens, being the second state to grant this right. The first state was also a western state, Wyoming. Perhaps out West it was easier for women to escape society's constraints. Here, only the hardiest and independent could be truly happy. I was among the first in line to vote in the following year's election and helped elect three women to the state legislature.

The same year also brought the Silver Panic. Fortunately, the mines around Ouray had always carried a certain amount of gold, overlooked when the silver prices were high. The Denver and Rio Grande Railroad also helped make it more profitable to ship ore of lower grade. With the arrival of electricity, productivity also increased. It was an Irishman, however, that set Ouray's fate from going the way of other mining ghost towns. Thomas Walsh made the fortunate discovery of Camp Bird Mine in 1896 when he was on the verge of bankruptcy. He purchased several existing mines and began staking claims in the vicinity. Quietly, he began to make a fortune from the gold-laden ore, which produced four million dollars over a span of five years.

With six children bustling about on our ranch, there was never a dull moment. I remember the day ten-year-old Annie ran up to me in the garden, crying at the top of her lungs. Once I realized she wasn't hurt, I tucked her head under mine and gave her a big mama-bear hug. Annie was a child who needed her mother's full attention before she'd settle down. "Now tell me what's bothering you, Annie."

"Henry says I can't rope," she sniffled. "Because I'm a little girl. Is that true, Ma?" Her brown eyes held mine fast.

I smiled and took her hand in mine. "We'll see about that." We walked out to the corral beyond the far side of the house. "Annie, wait

Maggie's Way

here a moment." I strode to the far side of the enclosure, where Henry adjusted the cinch on his saddled horse. "Hello, Son. Going for a ride?"

"Naw, just going to work on my roping."

"Henry, why did you tell Annie she couldn't rope?"

"Ma, she could get hurt." He placed one hand at his waist and cocked his head. "If she managed to get the rope around a calf's neck, it'd drag her right to the ground and clear across the corral."

I softly placed a hand on his shoulder, which now stood level with mine. "Henry, how old were you when you started learning how to rope?"

"Oh, about eight, I think."

"I believe that a gal with a good teacher — one who might show her a few tips — would do just fine." I gave him a knowing smile.

Henry sighed. "Okay, Ma. I'll help her."

"That's my young man." I kissed him on the cheek and looked back to see Annie grinning for all her worth.

In the year 1901, Thomas Walsh was pointed out to me as he sat dining in the back of Ma's restaurant. This dignified, dapper Irishman proved a respected member of the community. From all I learned, he never forgot his own hardworking days. He treated his miners with such consideration that, when the labor troubles arose throughout the San Juans at the turn of the century, there were never any problems at his mines. He insisted on treating his men with justice and believed good food, clothing, and medical treatment were the due of all miners. Always proud to boast of my Irish blood despite commonly held prejudice, it was satisfying to find the man was held in such high regard. I tried to watch him inconspicuously as I served my brood of children. How surprised I was when, after paying for his meal, he strode over to our table.

"Have I been informed correctly that you are the former Maggie O'Malley?"

"Yes," I said. I was at a loss for words as I watched the man with the neatly trimmed moustache.

He held out his hand in greeting. I shook it firmly.

"It's an honor to meet the infamous lady mule skinner of the San Juans. You know, you're nearly a legend among the miners."

At last I found my voice.

"I'm sure it's hard to believe those stories by looking at the current chapter of my life." I nodded my head toward the large table of children.

"Not at all, my dear. Your good Irish inheritance proves your strength and versatility. You can drive mules, cattle, or children. Only a good Irish lass could handle all of that."

A sudden boom of good-hearted laughter arose from the nearby tables. It seems all eyes had been on Thomas Walsh and me throughout the conversation.

"Good day, my dear."

"Ma, who was that?" fifteen-year-old James asked, wide-eyed.

"Mr. Walsh, the owner of the Camp Bird Mine."

Eleven-year-old Annie chimed in at that point.

"Ma, did you hear him say you're *famous?*" She was astounded at the thought that her ordinary old mother was the subject of miner's folklore.

"Well, famous might be a bit overplayed, but I suppose I did have my day of adventure."

Little Margaret stared at me as if she had never heard her father tell the stories of her mother's days of freighting. To a young child, I suppose, a stranger can give more credibility than one's own parent.

47

1915

How the years have flown! Matthew and I remained alone at the home place, for all the children were grown. Our ranching had become quite an enterprise, supporting the children who remained to work the ranch along with us. Joshua, Thomas, and Henry all had families now and built their own homes within a fifteen-mile radius of the "old folks." James attended a seminary back East but insisted he would return West when finished. Like his father, he felt a calling to preach the gospel. Annie married a young banker in Ouray several years ago, much to the delight of my mother. Margaret returned home from Denver and lived up to her namesake: she had become a veterinarian. With the help of her brothers, she built her own cabin in the Ridgway area, where she planned to practice her trade. Some of her brothers worried that she was getting too old to marry. I smiled, knowing where her independent spirit came from. I believed she would find the right man, not unlike her own father, who would appreciate her high spirits. Our growing family provided Matthew and me with thirteen grandchildren. How Ma's little family had expanded! She delighted in all her grandchildren and great-grandchildren, bragging to all of Ouray of her fine family.

Having turned fifty-seven years old my last birthday, I thought myself a seasoned western woman who could handle anything. How false was my bravado. I will always remember the young man running up to me after Sunday service in Placerville. I recalled he worked at the telegraph office. With my whole soul frozen, I stared at the paper thrust into my hand and refused to open it. Telegrams were usually bad news.

I stood stunned until Matthew walked over, noticing something amiss. He took the message from my hand, read it, and then walked me over under a tree where we sat down. I searched his face then, waiting. His eyes misted up, and I prayed it was not bad news about James, so far from home, or Annie, who was due to deliver the end of the month.

"It's your mother, Maggie. She's gone."

I stood up.

"No! She's strong and healthy," I shouted. "She would never leave me like this. Matthew, go to the telegraph office. There's been a horrible mistake."

"Maggie, she's gone."

"No, you're wrong!"

Then, despite my fifty-seven years, my legs ran like a young girl's, carrying me down to the river away from all the gawking people who had not yet left for home after the service. Matthew let me go. After ten minutes, he found me sobbing at the water's edge further down the length of the river.

He stood next to me, for once not touching me, waiting silently. My head drooped, staring at the grass striking up from the red soil.

"Oh, Matthew. What will I do without her?"

When no response was forthcoming, I looked up to find Matthew weeping.

"She became my mother, too."

We alternately reminisced about Ma's life and cried. After some time, we walked back up to our horses. News spread quickly. There stood our little congregation and half the town, respectfully removing hats as we passed by. Words were not necessary. There would be a time for that later.

It was one of the largest funerals Ouray ever witnessed. All businesses closed that morning out of respect for one of the first businesswomen of the mining town. I knew my mother was loved by many, yet it was still overwhelming to see the turnout. Our family alone filled the first five rows at the church, what with so many grandchildren and spouses. Only James, who regretted missing his grandma's funeral, was absent, but there was no way he could travel home in three days, even by train. Townspeople stood in the back of the church, spilling out to the street.

My children had deeply loved their grandma, having spent so much time with her. It was a dismal day for us. If the service had been held in a saloon, as they were so many years before, it would have deserved the name "Bucket of Tears," as many were shed that day by both family and friends alike.

Matthew and I sat somberly in the front row of the chapel. Annie sat next to me, her husband, John, sitting beside her. She leaned into me, crying softly throughout most of the service. Living in Ouray, Annie had become very close to her grandma. They often shopped and sewed together, partook of tea many afternoons, and dined at each other's homes. Tender-hearted Annie would feel the gaping loss of her grandmother for a long time to come.

That evening, our family, with all the wives, husbands, and little ones, gathered at Annie and John's two-story columned house. After dinner was over, the women cleaned up in the kitchen, and the smallest children were put to sleep on deep feather beds in the many bedrooms of the large house. Then we all gathered in the parlor. Matthew helped Annie pass out hot mulled cider.

Joshua, taller than his father now, tapped the side of his glass to gain the attention of our loquacious clan. His handsome, strong-angled face lit up as he recalled how Grandma had taught him to cook. When he was five, she had brought out her baking tin, and together they had ventured outdoors to make a gooey mud cake.

"Grandma coerced me into tasting our creation," he said. "After I grimaced like a sick coyote, I spit the 'batter' out over a five-foot span. Then she wiped the corners of my mouth with the end of her apron and treated me to a huge piece of her freshly baked fudge cake." Joshua sat down on the sofa — then, on second thought, got to his feet again. "And I've never cooked again to this day." Laughter erupted in the room.

Margaret, her grandmother's namesake and the child most like my mother in character, rose to her feet. Her auburn hair bound in a thick braid hung in contrast to the unadorned black dress. A simple, natural beauty, the young woman was oblivious to the charm she exuded.

"You know how fastidious Grandmother was about her kitchen," she said, her green eyes taking in the faces of all in the room. "She once allowed me to bring a stray cat into O'Malley's restaurant."

Several chuckles were heard and a couple of heads shook in disbelief. All knew of Margaret's compulsion to take in stray or injured animals and birds over the years.

"She allowed me to bring the weak, scruffy cat inside. The poor thing had met with the worst end of a tomcat ruckus." Margaret made special eye contact with the children sitting in the center of the floor. Their eyes wide, the older children sat enraptured as they listened to the tale. "The poor tom," Margaret continued, "had a crimson-stained gouge in his side. I studied Grandmother carefully as she cleansed the wound and stitched it up with ordinary sewing thread. That cat's wound healed like thick cowhide. I credit Grandmother with my decision to become a veterinarian." She sat down. Hands came together in applause.

Maggie's Way

The other two boys told of their escapades and memories of my mother. Matthew stood by my side, his arm wrapped around my shoulders. Throughout the stories, he would kiss my temple or lean his face against mine. I looked around the room and saw many eyes shining like morning dew, even in my grown boys, despite the frequent laughter.

Joshua rose, his glass raised for a toast. His face somber, his blue eyes misty, he had the gentlest heart of all my boys. "To a grand lady," he declared, "whom we all loved. We'll carry her in our hearts always."

"To Grandmother." The glasses clinked melodiously as we celebrated my mother's life.

I was glad my mother did not die after a lingering illness, but I regretted not getting to say goodbye to her. I spent the next six months doing that in a spiritual sense. She was eighty years old that year and died stirring an Irish stew in her kitchen while humming a melody. By the time she hit the floor, she had already left this earth. She would have preferred to go exactly the way she did.

She was a grand lady . . . a great mother, an amazing grandmother, but she also extended herself to many other people. How many lives did she lighten, how many people did she help with a ready ear, a much-needed meal, or even her hard-earned money? Her life was a great example to all of our family, and we would sorely miss our Irish matriarch.

But, most of all, she was my mother, and I felt like an orphaned child for a long time after her death.

FULL MOON, HONEYMOON

Young people think life is over when old age comes, but for some it is only beginning. It took a few years before I fully came to terms with Ma's death. After that, a new stage in my life arose, like the violet penstemon blooming after a long winter. Perhaps because I knew now how brief and precious life was, a special chapter in my marriage began.

Although we were both beginning to feel the aches and pains that accompany aging bodies, Matthew and I still rode horseback across the meadows. The never-ending work of raising a large herd had been handed over to our sons like a torch in an ancient Olympic race. Each week we visited our children and grandchildren, alternating which family we would stop to see. Respectfully, the boys listened to Matthew's advice and hard-won experience from over the years.

Once a month Matthew still preached in Placerville. He was a beloved fixture in the small community, but he discerned it was time to let one of the young men take over the rest of the services and the growing work of calling on members in need.

This time in our lives became a honeymoon period for us. By now, of course, we knew each other so well we were finishing each other's sentences, but the tenderness and humor of our marriage ever increased. The busy years of working and raising children had ended. We found ourselves acting as young people again, despite the mirror that proclaimed otherwise. We indulged in frequent picnics during fair weather. Even yet, we sometimes dipped a pan in the creek looking for color, but no longer with an appetite for sudden wealth. We had all the blessings in life any couple could have asked for, and we were now more than content.

We hunted for an occasional deer or rabbit, enjoying nature more than the hunt, knowing our sons would happily bring a side of beef whenever needed. We savored a meal of good venison steak or fried rabbit served with homemade biscuits or cornbread, tea, and wild raspberries, when we could find them. We delighted in seeing the diversity of wildlife on our afternoon rides. Over the years, we never tired of glimpsing a black bear in the distance, a lynx scuttling out of harm's way, eagles in their effortless flight high above, or a hawk's smooth ride on the air currents.

In the autumn, we thrilled at watching bull elk in rut, clanging their large racks at one another in competition over the cows.

We revived a part of our relationship we had never totally lost: the art of play. Our children would tell stories of catching us in a water fight in the creek on a hot summer day, or of seventy-year-old Matthew picking a bouquet of wildflowers for their mother while out walking with one of his sons. On summer evenings, we liked to sit outside by the campfire and watch the stars overhead as we once did when we were building our cabin. The difference was, we now wrapped up together under a wool blanket as we drank our cup of tea. Our adult children shook their heads in amazement the day we made mud pies with the grandchildren.

What they don't know is how an old couple still held each other close at night, often falling asleep in each other's arms, thanking God for the good fortune of meeting.

EPILOGUE

The man stopped to remove his hat and wipe the sweat from his brow. The temperature was warm for this altitude, seeming even hotter yet after the consistently cool working conditions below in the mine. Albert's eyes squinted to adjust to the drastic degree of light above ground. He rubbed them and wondered if they served him right, for in the distance came a rider with two waist-length braids, white as the San Juan peaks in winter. An old Indian, he wondered? Joe, a young miner beside him, suddenly gave a holler and ran up to the rider.

"The mail's here," he yelled for the sake of anyone in hearing distance.

Albert walked over to the rider who was now dismounting, despite the fact that there was no one left to send mail to him. Several others who did, in fact, expect mail shuffled out of the boarding house. A couple of men, probably with sweethearts, bypassed Albert in their exuberance. He stood at a slight distance studying the mail carrier. The rider's head lifted to reveal an aging face below the weathered hat. By God, it was an old woman! The old hen had ridden clear up the mountain just to deliver the mail. She seemed to be familiar with a few of the men, who affectionately called her "Ma" or "Grandma." He thought he heard the old Irishman call her "Maggie."

Soon the men who had received mail were off to read their prized letters, while the remaining dispirited souls ambled off. Only Albert and an old miner lingered. Albert watched the old woman mount her horse and turn back down the mountain. He noted a hammer hung from her saddle horn and what looked like the handle of a pick sticking out of one of the leather saddlebags. A minor detail that caught his eye was the crude rope threaded through the belt loops on the trousers.

"That poor old woman must be down and out if she has to resort to delivering mail way up here." He spoke to the old man as he stood watching her ride off in the distance. The men had nicknamed him "Irish." The old guy turned to Albert and shook his head.

"That lady is actually quite wealthy; her sons run a huge cattle business that she started years ago with her husband. Her old man, though, passed away six months ago — died in his rocking chair overlooking their land one evening. Died holding her hand as she sat beside him, never knew what happened to him. That's the way I'd like to go." Irish looked off into the distance, despite the fact the rider had long disappeared.

Albert considered what he had been told, wondering what kind of rich woman would choose such an occupation so late in life when she could be home sitting and rocking, or tending a flower garden.

"Do you suppose she went a little mad after her old man passed on? What's wrong with her family to allow this?" Albert usually spoke little to the men, preferring to keep to himself, but his curiosity had gotten the best of him.

Irish gave a chuckle.

"Suppose they know the fastest way to kill her would be to keep her at home doing nothing. She's lived her whole life in the hills, loving the mountains. Guess you don't know, but that lady is a real legend around these parts. Sit down a minute, and I'll tell you about the toughest little Irish mule skinner ever roamed the San Juans."

Albert took a seat on a nearby stump, eager for more of the story.

Decades later, a couple walked the hills above an area they had recently purchased. They planned to build a new rambling vacation home on the site. They were ready for a full afternoon of hiking, and were equipped with water bottles, a compass, cell phone, and a BLM map, in case their city ways proved inadequate for the wilderness. After walking for an hour, they decided to catch their breath under a glimmering stand of aspens.

"This is a beautiful view from here," the woman commented.

"We can spend every summer vacation here," the man said. "If you invite your folks, we could do holidays here, too."

"I still can't believe our good luck."

"Well, Carey, I wouldn't exactly call it luck. I've worked my tail off for years to get where we are today," the man said, offended.

Carey reached over and kissed him on the temple.

"I know, dear. It's just such a dream come true."

He held her hand. The offense was forgiven.

"Bill, what's that over there under the trees?"

"I'm not sure, can't make it out from here," he said.

"Let's explore!" Carey grabbed his hand.

Maggie's Way

The couple wandered under the aspen grove where sunlight dappled over grass and wildflowers.

"There was some sort of building here once," Bill stated, assessing the ground where a stone foundation remained.

He walked around in an ever-widening perimeter, finding the hidden remains of smaller outbuildings. He came back to the stone foundation and stepped over it, sifting through the leaves and long grasses with the toe of his hiking boot. A rusted metal pipe lay beneath some flowering columbines. He knew the name of the flowers only because he had seen a photo of them in a travel brochure. He believed they were the state flower. From the stovepipe and a nearby rusted tin cup, he concluded this had to be the relics of an old house.

"Bill, come here!" Carey shouted.

He hurried over, hoping she had not spooked a skunk or, worse, cornered a badger. Carey pointed to the granite stone.

"I think I've discovered who lived here."

She knelt down and brushed aside the long grasses that veiled the engraved inscriptions on the stone. She reached into the pocket of her shorts, pulled out a tissue, and wiped away the grime.

Bill leaned on one knee beside her, peering at the weathered lettering. "Now Reunited in our Father's Heaven. Matthew Harding 1853-1923, Man of God and loving husband and father. Margaret O'Malley Harding 1858-1933, Our loving mother now roams the hills with God."

The couple stood. Hand in hand, they walked back down the mountain in silence.